DAYENU

Dayenu

and Other Stories

James Sallis

n
e
w
RIVERS
PRESS
MSUM

©2021 by James Sallis
First Edition
Library of Congress Control Number: 2019956991
ISBN: 978-0-89823-401-5
e-ISBN: 978-0-89823-402-2

New Rivers Press is a nonprofit literary press associated with Minnesota State University Moorhead.

Cover design by Mallory McEachran
Interior design by Nayt Rundquist
The publication of *Dayenu and Other Stories* is made possible by the generous support of Minnesota State University Moorhead, the Dawson Family Endowment, and other contributors to New Rivers Press.

MINNESOTA STATE UNIVERSITY
MOORHEAD.

NRP Staff: Nayt Rundquist, Managing Editor; Kevin Carollo, Editor; Travis Dolence, Director; Trista Conzemius, Art Director
Interns: Gabbie Brandt, Dana Casey, Alex Ferguson, Katie Martinson, Delaney Noe, Olivia Rockstad

Dayenu and Other Stories book team: Mercedez DeWald, Hannah Heitz, Dorothy Pihlaja

∞ Printed in the USA on acid-free, archival-grade paper.

Dayenu and Other Stories is distributed nationally by Small Press Distribution.

New Rivers Press
c/o MSUM
1104 7th Ave S
Moorhead, MN 56563
www.newriverspress.com

Contents

How the Damned Live On

The closest I can come to the giant spider's name is Mmdhf. She loves to talk philosophy. How we become what and who we are, why we are here, the influence of the island's isolation on what we believe. She waits for me each morning on the beach. As I approach along the steep, snaking path from the cave, I imagine paper cups of coffee at the end of two of her arms. They steam in the early morning chill.

"You slept well?" she asks.

"I did."

I tell her about the dreams. In the latest versions I find myself lost on the streets of a teeming city. No one will respond to my pleas for help. Then I ask: "Do you dream?"

"Another of your difficult questions. We sleep, and live within the sleep. Perhaps we—my kind, I mean—fail to differentiate between the two lives."

Pirates come in the night and carry off all our things: spare clothing and blankets, the crate of fig preserves, sharp knives, our half-built raft. Later we see they have used material from the last to repair the deck and railings of their ship.

◿

There are flowers and plants here like none we have ever seen, vast thickets of them awash with colors one might more reasonably anticipate finding in tropical climes, some of the flowers aloft on stems high above our heads. Cook fears one of the lesser plants. He insists that they uproot themselves and move around at night, that he lies awake listening to the soft pad of their rootsteps. Anything is possible, the Professor responds.

They are both wrong, I hope.

Ahmad meanwhile is at wit's end. He does not know in what direction Mecca might be.

◿

Captain stands for hours at a time, statuelike, alone on the open beach where we washed ashore, sextant aimed to the heavens. He has long ago given up on his charts. They lie abandoned in a far recess of the cave. Increasingly, when we speak to him his replies seem insensible.

I ask Mmdhf one morning the name of the island, what she calls this, her home. Thoughtfully she speaks the word in her language, a long word that rolls on and on in her barbed, glistening mouth. It might best be translated, she tells me, as This Place.

The pirates, it appears, have mutineed, discharging their captain, complete with parrot, onto the island. The parrot and Mmdhf have become close. They sit all afternoon beneath a favored banyan tree talking. I am beginning to feel, as I suspect the pirate captain must, jealous.

◢

Each incoming wave washes tiny, fingernail-sized crabs onto the shore, dozens of them. They weigh almost nothing, what a heavy breath weighs, perhaps. Their shells and flesh are transparent. As the water recedes they take their bearings, right themselves, and scuttle towards the sea. A few make it. Most are driven back onto the shore by the next wave.

◢

Long ago Mmdhf explained to me how so many of her children had died, all of them actually, and that this is what brought her to a deeper thinking. It was then (how had I not known this before?) that I understood she was the last and only one of her kind.

◢

Our subsistence, the subsistence of most all the island's life forms, depends upon a fruit we call Tagalong, which also serves as substitute womb for the island's most common insect, a horned, armored species resembling a cigar that has sprouted legs. These lay their eggs in the Tagalong. Commonly one bites into the fruit to discover a larval head peering out.

Tagalong grows most abundantly towards the center of the island—due, the Professor says, to the dormant volcano there, its creation of a temperate zone. For the same reason, and for ready access to quantities of Tagalong, birds flock to the area in vast numbers. Of late, birds have begun to move away. This suggests, the Professor tells us, that the volcano is about to erupt.

The parrot agrees.

∆

Mmdhf and I have spoken daily for months when I come to realize that I find something in her speech unsettling. Her enunciation is perfect, her word choice spot on; she speaks without appreciable accent and with proper inflection. Yet something nips at the heels of our dialogues. My uneasiness, I decide at length, lies in subtle shadings of verb choices.

Is it possible, I ask one morning, that we experience time differently?

"As in our earlier discussion of dream and waking," she replies, "yes. And you cannot imagine how surprised I was to learn that time for your kind is not continuous but sequential."

"But if continuous, how can there be said to be time at all?"

"This." She turns her head, pauses, turns back. "Change."

"If all time is one . . ." I hesitate, groping for the question. ". . . then you know the future, you know what will happen."

"Yes." She lifts two legs, as I have seen her do only once before, when she spoke of her children. "I miss you."

◊

Miss Cruz

I think I always knew I didn't fit in. I'd look around at the families, their dogs and bikes and travel trailers, parents hopscotching cars out of the driveway every morning to go to work, and knew I'd never be a part of that. Most of us feel that way, I guess, when we're young. But with me it wasn't a matter of feeling. I knew.

The other thing I knew was that I needed secrets, needed to know things others didn't, have keys to doors that stayed locked a lot. When I was a kid, for two years all I could think or read about was magic tricks, this arcane stuff no one knew much about. Thurston's illusions, Chung Ling Soo, Houdini. Sleight of hand and parlor magic and bright lacquered cabinets. Read every book in the library, spent the little money I had on a subscription to a slick magazine named *Genie* out of L.A. Later it was Hawaiian music (can't remember how that got started), then 19th-century clocks. I was looking, you see, looking for stuff other people didn't know, looking for secrets. They were as essential to me as water and the air I breathed.

One thing I *didn't* know was that I'd wind up here in this desert, where it looks, as someone told me when I first came, like God squatted down, farted, and lit a match to it. Long way from the hills and squirrel runs I grew up in. Everything low and spread out, dun-colored and difficult. But hey, you want to build this big-ass city, how much better could you do than smack in a wasteland where it's a hundred degrees three months out of the year, and water, along with everything else, has to be trucked in?

But cities are like lives, I guess, when we start out, we never know what they're going to turn into. So here I am, living in what's politely termed a residential hotel on the ass-end side of Phoenix, Arizona, with half a dozen T-shirts, two pair of jeans, a week's worth of underwear if I don't leak too much, some socks, a razor, and a toothbrush. Oh—and a four-thousand dollar guitar. It's a Santa Cruz, black as night all over, not even any fret markers on her. Small, but with this huge sound.

Because I'm a musician, see. Have the black suit, white shirt, and tie to prove it. They're all tucked into one of those dry-cleaner bags in the back of what passes for a closet here. It's the size of a coffin; at night I hear things with bristly legs moving around in there. Outside the closet, there's half of what began life as a bunk bed, a table whose Formica top has a couple of bites out of it, two chairs, and a dresser with a finish that looks like maple candy.

And the guitar case, of course, all beat to hell. Same case I've had all along, came with the Harmony Sovereign I found under the bed in a rented room back in Clarksdale, Mississippi around 1980, when it all started. Second one, a pawnshop guitar, didn't have a case, so I kept this one, and after that . . . well, not much history or tradition in my life, you work with what you have. Been a lot of guitars in there since. Couple of J-45s, an old small-body Martin, a Guild archtop, Takamines, a Kay twice as old as I am. Really get some looks when I pull this gorgeous instrument out of that case. Books and covers, right?

I forgot to mention the stains on ceiling and mattress. Lot of similarities among them; I know, I've spent many a night and long afternoon sandwiched between, mattress embossed with personal stories, all those who fell to earth here before me, stains on the ceiling more like geological strata, records of climate changes, weather, cold winters and warm.

It's not a big music town, Phoenix. Mostly a big honking pool of headbangers and cover bands, but there's work if you're willing. What do I play? Like Marlon Brando in *The Wild Ones* said when asked what he was rebelling against: What do you have? Mariachi, Beatles tributes, polka, contra, happy-hour soft jazz—I've done it all. Even some studio work. But my bread and butter's country. Kind of places you find an ear under one of the tables as you're getting the guitar out of the case and the bartender tells you good, they've been looking for that, got torn off in a fight last weekend.

Those gigs, mostly Miss Cruz stays in the case, right there by me all night, and I play a borrowed Tele that belongs to . . . I started to say a friend, but that's not right. An associate? Man doesn't play, but he has this room with thirty or more guitars, all top drawer, and humidifiers pouring out fog everywhere so you go in there it's like stepping into a rain forest, you keep expecting parrots to fly out of the sound holes. Jason Fletcher. We work together sometimes. Secrets, remember? And he's a lawyer.

Thing is, musicians get around, hear things. We're on the street, out there wading in the sludge of the city's bloodstream. And we're like furniture in the clubs, no one thinks we're listening or paying attention or give half a damn. Plus, we get to know the barkeeps and beer runners, who see and hear more than us.

So I do a little freelance work for Jason sometimes. Started when he came by Bad Mojo down on the lower banks of McDowell looking for a client of his who owed him serious money and caught me with a pick-up band playing, of all things, Western Swing. Strong bass player/singer, solid drummer, steel player who'd been at it either two weeks or forty years, hard to tell. Anyhow, Jason and I got to talking on a break, and he said how he'd always wanted to play like that and wanted to know if I gave lessons. People are coming up to you all the time at gigs and asking that, so I didn't think much of it, but a few days later, comfortably late in the morning, my phone rang. After work that day he swung by, and when he opened up the case he was carrying, there was a kickass old Gibson hollowbody.

The lesson lasted about twenty minutes before dissolving into gearhead chatter. Man could barely play a major scale or barred minor chord, but he knew everything about guitars. Woods, inlay, model designations, who made what for whom, Ditson, Martin, the Larsons, Oscar Schmidt—had it all at his fingertips, everything but music.

"Were you mathematically inclined as a child?" I remember he asked. It was a question I'd heard before and, knowing where he was taking it, I said no, it's just pattern recognition: spatial relationships, forms. That musicians, all artists, are just compulsive pattern-makers at heart.

And like with music, you stay loose, follow where life takes you. You've got the head, the changes, but the tune's what you make of it, you find out what's in there. So when the lesson dismembered itself we went out for a beer and went on talking and the rest just kind of developed from there. He'd say keep an ear out for this or that, or once in a while something would drift my way that had a snap to it and I'd pass it along.

For the rest, I have to go back a year or so.

It's a breezy, cold spring and I'm sitting in the outdoor wing of a coffeehouse with half an inch left in my cup for the last half hour looking over at the café next door, Stitches, a frou-frou place heavy on fanciful salads and sandwiches. There's a waitress over there that just looks great. Nothing glamorous or even pretty about her, plain, really, a summer-dress kind of girl, but these sad, unguarded eyes and, I don't know, a presence. Also an awkwardness or hesitancy. She'll stall out by a table sometimes. Or you look over and she's just standing there—on pause, like, holding a plate or a rag or the coffee.

There are all kinds of ways of knowing things, and in the weeks I've been watching, it's become obvious that she and the manager are down. Nothing in the open, but lots of small tells for the watchful: their faces when they talk to one another, the way their bodies kind of bend away from one another when they pass, occasional glances into the relic'd mirrors set up like baffles all through the café.

Secrets. Things others don't know.

And in the past few days it's become just as obvious that it's over. They've had The Talk. She stalls out more often, gets orders wrong, forgets refills and condiments.

So, lacking much of an attention span and with a loose-limbed hold on reality, I'm sitting there, looking over, thinking how great it would be if she went calmly to the cooler behind the counter, grabbed a pie, walked up to him, and let him have it. Everyone over there in Stitches is staring. And the manager is standing stock still with meringue and peaches dripping off his nose.

All at once then I come to, back to my surroundings, to realize that I'm witnessing, with a half-second delay, exactly what I've been picturing in my mind.

Now *that's* interesting.

Sweat runs down my back as I wonder how far I can take this.

One of the other waitresses runs into the kitchen, comes back with a can of whipping cream, and lets him have it in the face, right there by the peaches. A few customers look upset, but most are laughing. The cooks come out, stand around him, and sing Happy Birthday. Then I have everybody hold still, like a picture's just been taken, then they move, then I stop them again, another picture.

Cool.

Then I get scared and bolt.

That night at a club called Tip's I sat down with my guitar and ran an E chord into an A as many ways as I could think of all over the neck, but that was it. After fifteen or twenty minutes, without saying anything, I put the guitar back in its case and left. Didn't play for weeks, didn't go out in public at all, really, just hung in my room. The pictures of those people in the restaurant doing what I was imagining in my mind, *exactly* what I was imagining in my mind, those stayed with me. But like pictures on a wall, eventually you get used to them, stop seeing them when you walk past. So after a while I eased on back into the world. I'd like to say I was strong enough or scared enough never to repeat the incident, never to take that song for another ride, but of course I wasn't.

Miss Cruz came to live with me not long after that. She wasn't happy where she was—a common story: unloved and unappreciated, neglect, abuse—and where *he* is, he has no need for her. His needs are pretty simple. They change the catheter every few days, squirt stuff in his eyes to keep them from drying out. I went there once to visit. Keep telling myself I didn't put him there, his own choices did—and that night he decided to beat up on his woman in the bar where I was playing.

This entire aspiring society, humankind itself, is built and maintained on violence. We all know that, but pretend we don't. What matters is when and against whom you let the dogs out, right?

So back now to Jason Fletcher, who'd shown up weeks before at a wine bar where I was playing a solo early-evening gig to tell me the sheriff's office was harassing his client and he'd appreciate my keeping ears open for anything that might help. Sheriff Jack Dean, a stump-legged rind of a man with a bad comb-over, long history of marginally legal activity, and continuous re-election by preying on fear. Fletcher's client had written an elaborately researched, clear-eyed series about him for the Republic and now found himself followed by unmarked cars wherever he went. Waiting outside his house in the morning, parked across from the coffee shop where he stopped on the way to work.

"These boys are slick from years of practice," Fletcher said, "they've got it down to a fine art. No marks, no bruises."

What came to me, what I picked up off the forest floor, wasn't all that much, but it worked. The guy was able to drink his coffee in peace, rumors of lawsuits and worse evaporated, no more was heard of the "inquiry" that had sheriff's men knocking on neighbor's doors.

It haunted me, after. I looked up the journalist's series in the Republic, read every word and climbed over every comma twice. Dropped in with ears open at a downtown bar frequented by cops. Understand, I'm not the kind ever to pay much heed to politics. Never thought about how rotten the whole thing was, or much cared. And if I did, simply assumed that corruption and greed had to be the universal standard. It's politics, right? And politics is about power, so how else could it be played? As for me, I just wanted to be left alone, to play my guitar, make music. But that whole sheriff thing wouldn't let go of me, kept nipping at my heels, pissing on my shoes. Who can say why it is some things stick to us? I'd be sitting in OK Coffee or 5&10 Diner, see a county car pull in, or some beat-up dude staggering by outside, and it would all start back up.

Something growing in the dark within me.

Then one night it's 4 a.m. after a free-jazz gig with a sax player, music with a lot of anger inside, and the anger comes home with me. One of those nights when moonlight's spilling everywhere, then clouds slide in and it goes dark. No wind, no breeze—like the world's stopped breathing. Neighbors somewhere playing what sounds like Texas conjunto on the radio. I'm rattling around the room like always after gigs, drained and dog-tired but still wired, cranked up to the very edge, when there's a change in the light, a flicker, and I look up at the TV. I've had it on with no sound, silent company in the night. *Breaking News*, the screen reads now. I turn up the sound.

There's been a huge raid on a houseful of illegals out near the county hospital. Clips show a dozen or more half-dressed adults and kids being loaded into vans. Peace officers and TV crew outnumber them three to one. Lights worthy of a movie set. Then a cut—live!—to the man himself, Sheriff Jack, at his desk, American flag at parade rest behind him. Hard at the helm even at this hour, working as ever (he tells us) to uphold the laws of the land, serve the good people of Maricopa County, defend every border, and keep us all safe.

Not a single word about profiling, illegal traffic stops, unwarranted search and seizure, rampant intimidation, financial irregularities, or the ongoing federal investigation of his department.

As he speaks, he touches his nose again and again, age-old tell of the liar. Third or fourth time, he takes the finger away, looks at it a moment, and sticks it *in* his nose. He's digging around in there. Still talking, talking, talking.

And I realize that what I just saw, the nose touch, the nose pick, I pictured in my mind half a moment before it happened.

Sheriff Jack pulls the finger out, examines it, and tries the other nostril.

I'm thinking okay, so I don't have to be there, looks like I just have to see it, as the good sheriff, never for a moment ceasing his recitation, drops down in a squat and duckwalks across the office floor, a full-bore Chuck Berry, cameraman struggling to change headings, go with the flow.

Escalations are taking place. In what the sheriff is doing, the brutal comedy of it. In the ever-increasing alarm stamped on his face: wild eyes, frantic silent appeals stage left and right. In my anger, growing by the moment. In the anything-but-comedy of my horrible pride at the power of what I can do.

Again that half-moment delay, that temporal stutter. Eyes wide, face twisted in alarm, just as I picture him doing in my mind, the sheriff draws his sidearm.

In my mind he places the sidearm to his temple.

Onscreen he places the sidearm to his temple.

He pauses. The moment stretches. Stretches.

In my mind he stops talking.

Dervishness then, confusion everywhere, as deputies rush in to scoop the sheriff up and bear him away.

I reached out to turn off the TV with hands shaking. Didn't sleep that night or for many nights to follow. Hardly left the apartment. Closed the door on what had happened, on what I could do, and have kept it shut, though every day when I turn the TV on, read the news, look around me at the mess of things, it gets harder. I answer the phone when calls come in, I go play my music, I come home. I keep my head down. I try real hard not to see things in my mind.

Mark Twain said a gentleman is someone who can play the banjo and doesn't.

So far, I've stayed a gentleman.

Ferryman

Let me say this: I'd stopped dating, stopped looking, stopped even fantasizing that the sexy young woman with tattoos at the local 7-Eleven where I bought my beer was going to follow me home. Still felt a gnawing loneliness, though, one that never quite went away and drew me out again and again, till I had a regular round of watering holes, places that exist outside the official version, largely unseen even by those who live near, part of the invisible city. Clinica Dental, for instance.

On any given day there you look out windows to see saguaro that grow for 75 to 100 years before the first arm comes along, and inside to see 99% Hispanic faces. Color and facial features ambiguous, Spanish serviceable as long as things stay simple, I don't stand out. And I'm not there for free dental care, which makes it easier, I'm just there to be in the flow, to climb out of my own head and place in the world for a look around.

Airports, bus stations, parks—all are great for that. But county hospitals and free clinics may be the best.

After a while I began to feel that I wasn't alone, that someone shared my folly. Like me, she blended in, but by the third or fourth glance, cracks started to show. Patients came and went—maids in uniform, yard workers, mothers with multiple kids in tow, an old guy that weighed all of eighty pounds lugging a string bass—and neither of us budged. From time to time, reading one of those self-help, motivational books with titles like *Find Happy* or *Say Yes to Your Dream* that turn out to be warmed-over common sense, she'd look up and smile. Now, of course, I understand book and visit for what they were: advanced research in how to pass.

When she left, I followed her on foot crosstown to Hava Java and lingered outside as she ordered. The place was busy, a jumble of young and old, hip and straight, some with lists of beverages to take back to the office, so she had a longish wait before staking out a table near the side window.

Two cups. Meeting someone, then.

But as I started to turn away, she beckoned, pointing to the second cup. I went in and sat. The kind of steel chair that looks great on paper but fits no part of the human body—legs too short, back at the wrong angle, seat guaranteed to find and grind bones. A young woman, evidently mute, went from table to table carrying a cardboard sign.

PLEASE HELP
HOMELESS
SPARE CHANGE?

When my tablemate held out a ten-dollar bill, their eyes met for half a beat before the woman took it, bowed her head, and moved away.

"Es café solo," my companion said, gesturing to the cup before me, "espero que esté bien."

Given my skin color and where we just were, a fair assumption. "Perfect," I said.

Seamlessly she shifted to English. No taint of accent in her voice. She could easily have been from the Midwest, from Washington state, from California. I noted the lack of customary accoutrements. No purse or backpack, no tablet, no cell phone in its holster. Just the book and a wallet with, presumably, money and ID. I noted also how closely she observed everything: figures passing in the world outside, the low buzz escaped from earphones at a table close by, a couple leaning wordlessly in towards one another. Had I ever known someone so content to let silence have its place, someone uncompelled to fill every available space with sound?

◢

Natalie was like that. Three or four weeks after we got together, we'd planned a weekend trip to El Paso and she came out of the house that morning at six, smell of new citrus in the air, with a backpack you could get a small lunch and maybe a pair of underwear in.

"That's it?" I said.

"Like to stay light on my feet. You?"

My now-shamed suitcase was in the trunk.

Light eased itself gingerly above the horizon as we moved through Natalie's battered neighborhood. The first three entrances onto I-10 were jammed. The city had grown too fast—a six-foot man on a child's playhouse chair. Too many bodies shipping in from elsewhere, riding the wagons of their dreams westward, northward.

This was the girlfriend who told me I didn't communicate, that I shut myself off from everyone and, when I shrugged, said, "See?" But that was later.

Of the trip mostly what I remember is driving along the river one evening on our way to dinner and the best chile relleno I ever had, looking over at shanties clustered on the bluff above and thinking how could anyone possibly expect that these people wouldn't try to cross over? Deliverance was right here, so easily visible, scant yards away. Reach out and you could touch it.

On that same trip, walking to breakfast the next morning, we found the bird's nest. I turned to say something and Natalie wasn't there. Two or three steps back, she was down on both knees.

"It must have fallen out. From up there." She pointed to a palo verde. "There's one broken egg shell."

She was almost to the point of tears as she picked the nest up, ran a finger gently along it. Twigs, pieces of vine, what looked to be string or twine, silvery stuff, grass or leaves.

"There's something here with words on it." She held the nest close to her face. "Can't make them out."

Across the street stood a Chinese restaurant, alley running alongside, dumpsters at the rear. I walked back for a better look at the nest. What she was seeing, intertwined among the twigs and other detritus, were slips from fortune cookies.

That's also when I found out what Natalie read since, as it turned out, the backpack held more books than clothing. When she moved in not long after, she brought a sack of jeans and t-shirts, ten stackable plastic bookshelves, two dozen boxes of science fiction paperbacks, and little else. Kuttner, Sturgeon, Emshwiller, Heinlein, Delany, Russ, LeGuin. I'd begun picking up the books she forever left behind in the bathroom, on the kitchen table, splayed open on counters, in the fissure between our shoved-together twin beds. Many had been read and reread so many times that you had to hold in pages as you made your way through. Before I knew it, I was hooked.

The books were all she took when she moved out, that and her favorite photo, a panoramic shot of the Sonoran Desert looking unearthly, lunar, forsakenly beautiful. Over the years I'd searched out copies of some of the books at Changing Hands and Bookmans. For the panorama I had only to drive a few miles outside the city bubble.

Not having been theretofore of an analytical turn of mind, nonetheless I came to recognize that, fulfilling as were these fantastic adventures in and of themselves, something far more substantial moved restless and reaching beneath the surface. The Creature swam in dark reverse of the woman in her white bathing suit above. Unsuspected worlds co-exist just out of frame and focus with our own. Transformations are a commonplace.

◁

The same transformations occur in memory, I know, and what I now recall is the two of us standing there looking at the bare expanse together. Natalie's photo of the Sonoran Desert, or the closest I could find to it—but it's her, my new brief companion, speaking.

"It looks as though it doesn't belong to this world."

"I often think that."

"Beautiful."

"Yes."

She moved closer. Our arms touched. Her skin was cold.

"Whatever lived there, on that world, its life would be spent in the pursuit of water. Certain plants would harbor water, water that could be harvested. When the blue moon came, always unpredictably, it would bring sudden, rapid rains. For an hour or two before the waters evaporated, shallow pools formed. . And hundreds of life forms would race towards those pools, fill them, congest them. They would overflow."

"That's quite a story—put together from almost nothing."

"Isn't that how we understand the world we find ourselves in, by stitching together bits and pieces of what we see?"

As we had climbed stairs to the apartment she asked what I did for a living and I explained that I worked here at home, nothing of great interest really, pretty much the high-tech equivalent of filing, staring at computer screens all day. How living all the time in your head can make you strange. That getting out among others on a regular basis helped. We'd wandered towards the computer as we talked. The desert photo was my screen saver.

I'd drawn the blinds partly closed when we entered. Sunlight slipped through them at an angle and fell in a rectangle on the desk, looking like a second, brighter screen.

"Eventually," she went on, "one species wins out in the race for water. For space and food. Drives the rest away or destroys them. But without them, without those others keeping the balance, that species can't survive. It crosses over, into a new land. It changes."

"And as with all immigrants, now everything becomes about fitting in, being invisible."

Quiet for a moment, she then said, "Becoming. Yes, exactly. It finds a way to go on."

Later I will remember Apollinaire, my mother's favorite poet: Their hearts are like doors, always doing business. I'll remember what Garrett, a friend far more given to physicality than I, wrote in one of his stories, describing intercourse: We were bears pounding salmon on rocks. And I will remember her face above me in early dawn telling me I would never be alone again.

Then she died.

I remember . . .

Within minutes there's a knock at the door. Dazed, I open it to find a man who looks exactly like her. There are others with him, a man and a woman who look the same. They come in, roll her body in bedspread and blanket Cleopatra-style, bear her away.

"Thank you," one of them says as they leave.

That morning I go for a long walk along the canal. I take little note of the water's slow crawl, of those who pass and pace me, of traffic on the interstate nearby, of the family of ducks who've made this their improbable home. I cannot say what I am feeling. Heartbreak. Shock. Pain. Loss. And at the same time . . .

Happiness, I suppose. Contentment.

Two weeks later I'm walking down the street on my way to coffee, peering up into trees for possible nests, when I hear the voice in my head. "Nice day," it says. "Maybe we could go for a walk along the canal later."

I've come to a stop with the first words, looking around, wondering about this voice, what's going on here—but of course I know. A father always knows. I was bringing a new life across.

⟋

Freezer Burn

Within a week of thawing Daddy out, we knew something was wrong.

He claims, seems in fact fully to believe, that before going cold he was a freelance assassin; furthermore, that he must get back to work. "I was good at it," he tells us. "The best."

When what he actually did was sell vacuum cleaners, mops and squeegee things at Cooper Housewares.

It doesn't matter what you decide to be, he's told us since we were kids, a doctor, car salesman, janitor, just be the best at what you do—one of a dozen or so endlessly recycled platitudes.

Dr. Paley said he's seen this sort of thing before, as side effects from major trauma. That it's probably temporary. We should be supportive, he told us, give it time. Research online uncovers article after article suggesting that such behavior in fact may be backwash from cryogenics and not uncommon at all, "long dreams" inherent to the process itself.

So, in support as Dr. Paley counseled, we agreed to drive Daddy to a meeting with his new client. How he contacted that client, or was contacted by him, we had no idea, and Daddy refused (certainly we'd understand) to violate client confidentiality or his own trade secrets.

The new client turned out to be not he but she. "You must be Paolo," she said, rising from a spotless porch glider and taking a step towards us as we came up the walk. Paolo is not Daddy's name. The house was in what we hereabouts call Whomville, modestly small from out here, no doubt folded into the hillside and continuing below ground and six or eight times its apparent size. I heard the soft whir of a servicer inside, approaching the door.

"Single malt, if I recall correctly. And for your friends?"

"Matilda, let me introduce my son—"

Immediately I asked for the next waltz.

"—and daughter," who, as ever in unfamiliar circumstances, at age twenty-eight, smiled with the simple beauty and innocence of a four-year-old.

"And they are in the business as well?"

"No, no. But kind enough to drive me here. Perhaps they might wait inside as we confer?"

"Certainly. Gertrude will see to it," Gertrude being the soft-voiced server. It set down a tray with whiskey bottle and two crystal glasses, then turned and stood alongside the door to usher us in.

I have no knowledge of what was said out on that porch but afterwards, as we drove away, Daddy crackled with energy, insisting that we stop for what he called a trucker's breakfast, then, as we remounted, announcing that a road trip loomed in our future. That very afternoon, in fact.

"Road trip!" Susanna's excitement ducked us into the next lane—unoccupied, fortunately. She must have forgotten the last such outing, which left us stranded carless and moneyless in suburban badlands, limping home on the kindness of a stranger or two.

Back at the house we readied ourselves for the voyage. Took on cargo of energy bars, bottled water, extra clothing, blankets, good toilet paper, all-purpose paper towels, matches, extra gasoline, a folding shovel.

"So I gotta know," Susanna said as we bumped and bottomed-out down a back road, at Daddy's insistence, to the freeway. "Now you're working for the like of Oldmoney Matilda back there?"

"Power to the people." That was me.

"Eat the rich," she added.

"Matilda is undercover. Deep. One of us."

Susanna: "Of course."

"In this business, few things are as they appear."

"Like dead salesmen," I said.

"*My* cover. And a good one."

"Which one? Dead, or salesman?"

"Jesus," Susanna said and, as if on cue, to our right sprouted a one-room church. Outside it sat one of those rental LED digital signs complete with wheels and trailer hitch.

COME IN AND HELP US HONE
THE SWORD OF TRUTH

Susanna was driving. Daddy looked over from the passenger seat and winked. "I like it."

"I give up. No scraps or remnants of sanity remain."

"Chill, Sis," I told her. "Be cool. It's the journey, not the destination."

"To know where we are, we must know where we're not."

"As merrily we roll along—"

"Stitching up time—"

Then *for* a time, we all grew quiet. Past windshield and windows the road unrolled like recalls of memory: familiar as it passed beneath, empty of surprise or anticipation, a slow unfolding.

Until Daddy, looking in the rear view, asked how long that vehicle had been behind us.

"Which one?" Sis said. "The van?"

"Yes."

"Well, I've not been keeping count but that has to be maybe the twenty-third white van since we pulled out of the driveway."

"Of all the cards being dealt," Daddy said, "I had to wind up with you jokers. Not one but two smart asses."

"Strong genes," I said.

"Some are born to greatness—"

"—others get twisted to fit."

"Shoes too large."

"Shoes too small."

"Walk this way . . ."

Half a mile further along, the van fell back and took the exit to Logosland, the philosophy playground. Best idea for entertainment since someone built a replica of Noah's ark and went bankrupt the first year. Then again, there's *The Thing* in Arizona. Been around forever and still draws. Billboards for a hundred miles, you get there and there's not much to see, proving yet again that anticipation's, like, 90% of life.

"They'll be passing us on to another vehicle," Daddy said. "Keep an eye out."

"Copy that," Susanna said.

"Ten-four."

"Wilco."

Following Daddy's directions, through fields with center-pivot irrigation rollers stretching to the horizon and town after town reminiscent of miniature golf courses, we pulled into Willford around four that afternoon. Bright white clouds clustered like fish eggs over the mountains as we came in from the west and descended into town, birthplace of Harry the Horn, whoever the hell that was, Pop. 16,082. Susanna and I took turns counting churches (eleven), filling stations (nine), and schools (three). Crisscross of business streets downtown, houses mostly single-story from fifty, sixty years back, ranch style, cookie-cutter suburban, modest professional, predominantly dark gray, off-white, shades of beige.

"You guys hungry?" Daddy said.

Billie's Sunrise had five cars outside and twenty or more people inside, ranging from older guys who looked like they sprouted right there on the stools at the counter, to clusters of youngsters with fancy sneakers and an armory of handhelds. Ancient photographs curled on the walls. Each booth had a selector box for the jukebox that, our server with purple hair informed us, hadn't worked forever.

We ordered bagels and coffee and, as we ate, Daddy told us about the time he went undercover in a bagel kitchen on New York's lower east side. "As kettleman," he said. "Hundred boxes a night, sixty-four bagels to the box. Took some fancy smoke and mirrors, getting me into that union."

Bagels date back at least four centuries, he said. Christians baked their bread, Polish Jews took to boiling theirs. The name's probably from German's *beugel*, for ring or bracelet. By 1700s, given as gifts, sold on street corners by children, they'd become a staple, and traveled with immigrant Poles to the new land where in 1907 the first union got established. Three years later there were over 70 bakeries in the New York area, with Local #338 in strict control of what were essentially closed shops. Bakers and apprentices worked in teams of four, two making the rolls, one baking, the kettleman boiling.

"So. Plenty more where that came from, all of it fascinating. Meanwhile, you two wait here, I'll be back shortly." Daddy smiled at the server, who'd stepped up to fill our cups for the third time. "Miss Long will take care of you, I'm sure. And order whatever else you'd like, of course."

Daddy was gone an hour and spare change. Miss Long attended us just as he said. Brought us sandwiches precut into quarters with glasses of milk, like we were little kids with our feet hanging off the seats. If she'd had the chance, she probably would have tucked us in for a nap. Luckily the café didn't have cupcakes. Near the end, two cops came in and took seats at the counter—regulars, from how they were greeted. Their coffee'd scarcely been poured and the skinny one had his first forkful of pie on the way to his mouth when their radios went off. They were up and away in moments. As they reached their car, two police cruisers and a firetruck sailed past behind them, heading out of town, then an ambulance.

Moments later, sirens fading and flashers passing from sight outside, Daddy slid into the booth across from us. "Everybody good?"

"That policeman didn't get to eat his pie," Susanna said.

"Duty calls. Has a way of doing that. More pie in his future, likely."

Smiling, Miss Long brought Daddy fresh coffee in a new cup. He sat back in the booth and drank, looking content.

"Nothing like a good day's work. Nothing." He glanced over to where Miss Long was chatting with a customer at the counter. "Either of you have cash money?"

Susanna asked what he wanted and he said a twenty would do. Carried it over and gave it to Miss Long. Then he came back and stood by the booth. "Time to go home," he said. "I'll be in the car."

We paid the check and thanked Miss Long and when we got to the car Daddy was stretched out on the back seat, sound asleep.

"What are we going to do?" Susanna asked.

We talked about that all the way home.

◇

Bright Sarasota Where the Circus Lies Dying

I remember how you used to stand at the window staring up at trees on the hill, watching the storm bend them, only a bit at first, then ever more deeply, standing there as though should you let up for a moment on your vigilance, great wounds would open in the world.

That was in Arkansas. We had storms to be proud of there, tornados, floods. All these seem to be missing where I am now—wherever this is I've been taken. Every day is the same here. We came by train, sorted onto rough-cut benches along each side of what once must have been freight or livestock cars, now recommissioned like the trains themselves, with eerily polite attendants to see to us.

It was all eerily civil, the knock at the door, papers offered with a flourish and a formal invocation of conscript, the docent full serious, the two Socials accompanying him wearing stunners at their belts, smiles on their faces. They came only to serve.

Altogether an exceedingly strange place, the one I find myself in. A desert of sorts, but unlike any I've encountered in films, books, or online. The sand is a pale blue, so light in weight that it drifts away on the wind if held in the hand and let go; tiny quartz crystals gleam everywhere within. At the eastern border of the compound, trees, again of a kind unknown, crowd land and sky. One cannot see through or around them.

They keep us busy here. With a failed economy back home and workers unable to make anything like a living wage, the government saw few options. What's important, Mother, is that you not worry. The fundamental principles on which our nation was founded are still there, resting till needed; our institutions will save us. Meanwhile I am at work for the common good, I am being productive, I am contributing.

That said, I do, for my part, worry some. This is the fourth letter I've written you. Each was accepted at the service center with "We'll get this out right away," then duly, weeks later, returned marked *Undeliverable*. It is difficult to know what this means, and all too easy to summon up dire imaginings.

To judge by the number and size of dormitories and extrapolating from the visible population, there are some four to five hundred of us, predominately male, along with a cadre of what I take to be indigenous peoples serving as support: janitorial, housekeeping and kitchen workers, groundsmen, maintenance. Oddly enough for this climate, they are fair, their skin colorless, almost translucent, hair of uniform length male and female. From dedicated eavesdropping I've learned bits and pieces of their language. It is in fact dangerously close to our own, rife with cognates and seemingly parallel constructions that could easily lead us to say, without realizing, something other than, even contrary to, what we intended.

The indigenes speak without reserve of their situation, of what they've achieved in being here, and not at all of what came before. They appear to relish routine, expectations fulfilled—to thrive on them—and to have little sense of theirs as lives torn away at world's edge, only jagged ends of paper left behind. Popular fiction would have me falling in love with one of them, discovering the true nature of the subjugation around me, and leading their people to freedom. Approved fiction, I suppose, would write of protagonist me (as someone said of Dosto-evsky's Alyosha) that he thought and thought and thought.

As I write this, recalling the failure of my three previous missives and a rare conversation with another resident here, I realize just how close we've come to a time when many will scarcely remember what letters are.

Kamil taught for years at university, one of those, I must suppose, composed of vast stone buildings and lushly kept trees whose very name brings to mind dark halls, and the smell of floor wax. Unable to settle ("like a hummingbird," he said), Kamil straddled three departments, music, literature, and history, weaving back and forth seeking connections. On a handheld computer he played for me examples of the music he'd employed in the classroom to elicit those connections from young people who knew little enough, he said, of any of the three disciplines, least of all history. Truth to tell, I wasn't able to make much of his music, but the title of one raucous piece, "Brain Cloudy Blues," stays with me.

I remember when you told me about circuses, Mother, the bright colors and animals, people engaged in all manner of improbable activities, the smells, the sounds, the faces, and then explained that they had gone away, there were no circus-es anymore, and the very last of what was left of them lay put away in storage in the old winter quarters of the greatest circus of all in a town faraway named Sarasota.

Are we all in Sarasota now? There are further chapters in my life, I know. What might they be like? When someone other than myself is turning the page.

The Beauty of Sunsets

I propped him in his chair with his arms on the desk and straightened his tie, a repp stripe upon which purples and grays had intermingled over the years, then reached across to his appointment calendar and on today's date, as I always did, stamped a tiny red skull. For decades Senator Prim had drained public money by the hundreds of thousands into private enterprises and vacation retreats, while steadfastly voting against safety nets or social welfare for the young, old, poor and infirm, meanwhile doing his part to strip every last thread of government support from education and the arts. He wouldn't be doing that anymore.

Not that I'm a big fan of paintings with drippy blocks of color or music that makes your back teeth ache, mind you, but I'll take them over grift and greed. As for education, don't think for a moment that I don't appreciate the job skills my government unwittingly gave me.

It was getting along towards day's end, light slanting in through blinds at the window and turning to bars of bright and dark on the floor. The senator's aide would be back in minutes from his daily trek to Xtreme Bean, by which time I'd be out on the street, back in the stew of humanity.

This was my last one. My job was done. I'd been paid, and now I'd taken down everyone on the list.

Blood sugar levels let me know I hadn't eaten for quite some time, so I found a place nearby, Bernie's, and took a seat at the end of the bar, ordering a draft and a pastrami sandwich. Probably not a lot they could do back in whatever passed as a kitchen to mess that up. The bartender was female. Bearing and gestures hovered between cute twenty-year-old and seen-it-all sixty. Dress, hair and visible accessories were a mix of can't-possibly-care and lumberjack. It worked.

On the TV suspended over the bar, yet another politician held forth on civic responsibility, deregulation, trickledown, gooby-gooby, gob-gob. One code word after another.

The pastrami tasted of rancid oil, as though it had sweated through a workout and gone unwashed. The beer glass had smudges and smears of soap (I hoped it was soap) along its sides.

"'Bout had my fill of that rot," the barkeep said, inclining her head toward the TV. She fished the remote out from under the bar, where they kept the shotgun in old westerns, and went rummaging through channels. An amateur sports event. Four barely literate people sitting around a table discussing celebrity divorces. A soap opera populated by tight-faced older women and young men with unruly hair. A couple of minutes towards the midpoint of *The African Queen*, Bogart slowly, subtly, surely becoming a different man.

Meanwhile, here outside the TV, in our get-along real world, something—a parade, another protest—went on outside. Sirens crossed and recrossed, heavy vehicles shouldered by, a loudspeaker on the move blared what appeared to be the same announcement over and again. At this distance, in here, its words were indistinguishable.

As business slowed to a saunter, then a crawl, possibly because I was the rare patron who hadn't heard it all before, the barkeep settled across from me to say how her old man has bad Alzheimer's and doesn't recognize her mother, doesn't even acknowledge she's there, and how glad her mother is about this, says it's the first time she's felt free in fifty-two years.

I finished my beer, left half the sandwich and a tip, and stepped outside. Hundreds of hurried, harried, unsmiling faces. The stew of humanity. Life has undone so many. Or is it that they—all of us, like Bogart, like the barkeep's mother—are forever on our way somewhere else? Are only *becoming*?

The sunset was well advanced, evening springing its many trapdoors. Back in the jungle, sunsets took your breath. The sky above so clear, smelling of water, of life. And now, here, this superb sunset lay about. It turned sky and earth red, poured fire into high windows, spoke of longing and of a quiet solace.

Is it possible that I actually felt my brain in the moment it changed, bright sparks scattering ceiling to floor as the world rebuilt itself within me? And in that moment I knew: what I had done for money all these years was but a beginning.

I was wrong. Senator Prim wouldn't be the last one. I had other appointments to keep. These would be on me.

What You Were Fighting For

I was ten the year he showed up in Waycross. It was uncommonly dry that year, I remember, even for us, no rain for weeks, grass gone brown and crisp as bacon, birds gathering at shallow pools of water out back of the garage where Mister Lonnie, a trustee from the jail, washed cars. And where he let me help, all the while talking about growing up in the shacks down south of town, bringing up four kids on what he made doing whatever piecemeal work he could find, rabbit stew and fried squirrel back when he was a kid himself.

I'd gone round front to fetch some rags we'd left drying on the waste bin out there and saw him pull in. Cars like that—provided you knew what to look for, and I knew, even then—didn't show up in those parts. Some rare soul had taken Mr. Whitebread's sweet-tempered tabby and turned it to mountain lion. The driver got out. He left the door open, engine not so much idling as taking deep, slow breaths, and stood in the shadow of the water tower looking around.

I grew up in the shade of that tower myself. There wasn't

any water in it anymore, not for a long time, it was as baked and broiled as the desert that stretched all around us. A few painted-on letters, an A, part of a Y, an R, remained of the town's name.

I could see Daddy inside, in the window over the workbench. Didn't take long before the door screeched in its frame and he came out. "Help you?" Daddy said. The two of them shook hands.

The man glanced my way and smiled.

"You get on back to your business, boy," Daddy told me. I walked around the side of the garage to where I wouldn't be seen.

"She's not handling or sounding dead on. And the timing's a hair off. Think you could have a look?"

"Glad to. Strictly cash and carry, though. That a problem?"

"Never."

"I'll open the bay, you pull 'er in."

"Yes, sir."

"Garrulous as ever, I see."

I went on around back, wondering about that last remark. Not too long after, Mister Lonnie finished up and headed home to his cell. They never locked it, and he had it all comfy in there, a bedspread from Woolworth's, pictures torn from magazines on the wall. You live in a box, he said, it might as well be a *nice* box. I went inside to the office, which was really just a corner with cinder blocks stacked up to make a wall along one side. Daddy's desk looked like it had been used for artillery practice. The chair did its best to throw you every time you shifted in it.

I was supposed to be studying but what I was doing was reading a book called *The Killer Inside Me* for the third or fourth time. I'd snitched it out of a car Daddy worked on, where it had slipped down between the seats.

Everyone assumed I'd follow in my father's footsteps, work at the tire factory maybe, or with luck and a long stubborn climb uphill become, like he had, a mechanic. No one called kids special back in those days. We got called lots of things, but special wasn't among them. This was before I found out why normal things were so hard for me, why I always had to push when others didn't.

They got to it, both their heads under the hood, wrenches and sockets going in, coming out. Every few pages I'd look through the holes in the cinder blocks. Half an hour later Daddy said the man didn't need him and he had other cars to see to. So the visitor went on working as Daddy moved along to a '62 Caddy.

After a while the visitor climbed in the car, started it, revved the engine hard, let it spin down, revved it again. Got back under the hood and not long after that said he could use some help. Said would it be okay to ask me, and Daddy grunted okay. "Boy's name is Leonard."

"You mind coming down here to give me a hand with this engine, Leonard?" the man said.

I was at a good part of the book, the part where Lou Ford talks about his childhood and what he did with the housekeeper, but the book would always be there waiting. When I went over, the man shook my hand like I was grown and helped me climb in.

"I'm setting the timing now," he said. "When I tell you, I need for you to rev the engine." He held up the timing light. "I'll be using this to—"

I nodded just as Daddy said, "He knows."

To reach the accelerator I had to slide as far forward in the seat as I could, right onto the edge of it, and stretch my leg out straight. I revved when he said, waited as he rotated the distributor, revved again. Once more and we were done.

"What do you think?" the man asked Daddy.

"Sounding good."

"Always good to have good help."

"Even for a loner, yeah."

The man looked back at me. "Maybe we should take a ride, make sure everything's tight."

"Or take a couple of beers and let the boy get to *his* work."

Daddy snagged two bottles from the cooler. Condensation came off them and made tiny footprints on the floor. I was supposed to be doing extra homework per my teachers, but what was boring and obvious the first time around didn't get any better with age. Lou and the housekeeper were glad to have me back.

Daddy and the man sat quietly sipping their beers, looking out the bay door where heat rose in waves, turning the world wonky.

"Kind of a surprise, seeing you here." That was Daddy, not given to talk much at all, and never one for hyperbole.

"Both of us."

Some more quiet leaned back against the wall waiting.

"Still in the same line of work?"

"Not anymore, no."

"Glad to hear that. Never thought you were cut out for it."

'Thing is, I didn't seem to be cut out for much else."

"Except driving."

"Except driving." Our visitor motioned with his bottle, a swing that took in the car, the rack, the tools he'd put back where they came from. "Appreciate this."

"Any time. So, where are you headed?"

"Thought I might go down to Mexico."

"And do what?"

"More of the same, I guess."

"The same being what?"

Things wound down then. The quiet that had been leaning against the wall earlier came back. They finished their beers. Daddy stood and said he figured it to be time to get on home, asked if he planned on heading out now the car was looking good. "You could stay a while, you know," Daddy said.

"Nowhere I have to be."

"Don't guess you have a place . . ."

"Car's fine."

"That your preference?"

"It's what I'm used to."

"You want, you can pull in out back, then. Plenty of privacy. Nothing but the arroyo and scrub trees all the way to the highway."

Daddy raised the rattling bay doors and the visitor pulled out, drove around. We put the day's used rags in the barrel, threw sawdust on the floor and swept up, swabbed the sink and toilet, everything in place and ready to hit the ground running tomorrow morn. Daddy locked up the Caddy and swung a tarp over it. Said while he finished up I should go be sure the man didn't need anything else.

He had the driver's door open, the seat kicked back, and he was lying there with eyes open. Propped on the dash, a transistor radio the size of a pack of cigarettes, the kind I'd seen in movies, played something in equal parts shrill and percussive.

"Daddy says to tell you the diner over on Mulberry's open till nine and the food's edible if you're hungry enough."

"Don't eat a lot these days."

He held a beer bottle in his left hand, down on his thigh. The beer must have been warm since it wasn't sweating. Crickets had started up their songs for the night. You'd catch movement out the corner of your eye but when you looked you couldn't see them. The sun was sinking in its slot.

"Saw the book in your pocket earlier," he said, "wondered what you're reading," and when I showed him he said he liked those too, even had a friend out in California that wrote a few. Everything there is about California is damn cool, I was convinced of that back then, so I asked a lot of questions. He told me about the Hispanic neighborhood he'd lived in. Billboards in Spanish, murals on walls, bright colors. Stalls and street food and festivals.

Years later I lived out there in a neighborhood just like that before I had to come back to take care of Daddy. It all started with him pronouncing words wrong. Holdover would be *holover*, or noise somehow turn to nose. No one thought much about it at first, but before long he was losing words completely. His mouth would open, and you'd watch his eyes searching for them, but the words just weren't there.

"Everyone says we get them coming up the arroyo," I said, "illegals, I mean."

"My friend? Wrote those books? He says we're all illegals."

Daddy came around to collect me then. Standing by the kitchen counter we had a supper of fried bologna, sliced tomatoes and leftover dirty rice. This was Daddy's night to go dancing with Eleanor, dancing being a code word we both pretended I didn't understand.

That night a storm moved toward us like Godzilla advancing on poor Tokyo, but nothing came of it, a scatter of raindrops. I gave up trying to sleep and was out on the back porch watching lightning flash behind the clouds when Daddy pulled the truck in.

"You're supposed to be in bed, young man," he said.

"Yes, sir."

We watched as lightning came again. A gust of wind shoved one of the lawn chairs to the edge of the patio where it tottered, hung on till the last moment, and overturned.

"Beautiful, isn't it?" Daddy said. "Most people never get to see skies like that."

Even then I'd have chosen *powerful*, *mysterious*, *angry*, *promise unfulfilled*. Daddy said *beautiful*.

It turned out that neither of us could sleep that night. We weren't getting the benefits of the weather, but it had a hold on us: restlessness, aches, unease. When for the second time we found ourselves in the kitchen, Daddy decided we might as well head down to the garage, something we'd done before on occasion. We'd go down, I'd read, he'd work and putter or mess about, we'd come back and sleep a few hours.

A dark gray Buick sat outside the garage. This is two in the morning, mind you, and the passenger door is hanging open. What the hell, Daddy said, and pulled in behind. No lights inside the garage. No one around that we can see. We were climbing out of the car when the visitor showed up, not from behind the garage where we'd expect, but yards to the right, walking the rim of the arroyo.

"You know you have coyotes down there?" he said. "Lot of them."

"Coyotes, snakes, you name it. And a car up here that ain't supposed to be."

"They won't be coming back for it."

"What am I going to see when I look under that hood?" Daddy glanced at the arroyo. "And down there?"

"About what you'd expect, under the hood. Down there, there won't be much left."

"So it's *not* just more of the same. I'd heard stories."

"I'm sorry to bring this on you—I didn't know. It's taken care of."

Daddy and the man stood looking at one another. "I was never here," the man said. "*They* were never here." He went around to the back. Minutes later, his car pulled out, eased past us, and was gone.

"We'd best get this General Motors piece of crap inside and get started tearing it down," Daddy said.

⊿

We all kill the past in our own way. Some slit its throat, some let it die of neglect.

Last week I began a list of species that have become extinct. What started it was reading about a baby elephant that wouldn't leave its mother's side when hunters killed her, and died itself of starvation. I found out that ninety percent of all things that ever lived on earth are extinct, maybe more. As many as two hundred species pass away between Monday's sunrise and Tuesday's.

I do wonder. What if I'd not been born as I was, what if I'd been back a bit in line and not out front, what if the things they'd told us about that place had a grain of truth. Don't do that much, but it happens.

"When the sun is overhead, the shadows disappear," my physical therapist back in rehab said. Okay, they do. But only briefly.

And: "At least you knew what you were fighting for." Sure I did. Absolutely. We steer our course by homilies and reductive narratives, then wonder that so many of us are lost.

A few weeks ago I made a day trip to Waycross. The water tower is gone, just one leg and half another still standing. It's a ghost town now, nothing but weightless memories tumbling along the streets. I pulled in by what used to be my father's garage, got my chair out and hauled myself into it, rolled with the memories down the streets, then round back to where our visitor had parked all those years ago. Nothing much has changed with the arroyo.

You always hear people talking about I saw this, I read this, I did this, and it changed my life.

Sure it did.

Thing is, I'd forgotten all about the visitor and what happened that night, and the only reason I remember now is because of this movie I saw.

I'd rolled the chair in at the end of an aisle only to be met with a barrage of smart-ass remarks about blocking their view from a brace of twenty-somethings, so I was concentrating on not tearing their heads off and didn't pay much attention to the beginning of the movie, but then a scene where a simple heist goes stupid bad grabbed my attention and I just kind of fell through the screen.

The movie's about a man who works as a stunt driver by day and drives for criminals at night. Things start going wrong then go wronger, pile up on him and pile up more until finally, halfway to a clear, cool morning, he bleeds to death from stab wounds in a Mexican bar. "There were so many other killings, so many other bodies," he says in voiceover near the end, his and the movie's.

After lights came on, I sat in the theater till the cleaning crew, who'd been waiting patiently at the back with brooms and a trashcan on rollers, came on in and got to work. I was remembering the car, his mention of Mexico, some of the conversation between my father and him.

I'm pretty sure it was him, his story—our visitor, my father's old friend or co-worker or accomplice or whatever the hell he was. I think that explains something.

I wish I knew what.

Dispositions

"Your child, the one you planned on naming Amelia, will be stillborn. The nurse practitioner and doctor will work for eighteen minutes to resuscitate her. She will never take a breath. Her tiny heart will not beat. They will clean the body and hand it to you. It will be limp and lifeless as a rag. You won't even be able to cry. I'm sorry."

Nor was she able to cry then, as her friend quickly took her arm and ushered her away. The woman looked lifeless herself as she was led off past a stationery-and-greeting-cards store towards Nordstrom's. In memory, in my mind, it seems that others parted right and left to let them pass.

"Fourteen thousand miles out beyond Pluto, which may or may not be a planet this week, there's a cosmic hole, a void, the size of our solar system," I tell Becca.

"Achh. The things we have to live with," Becca says, and pours coffee.

I tell her about the chairs. They were laid out for a wedding in 1939 in Poland. With the German invasion, the wedding was abandoned, and so were the chairs. They were found again after the war with the trees growing through them. Every year now they are repainted.

"What color?" she asks.

I tell her about the woman, the baby.

"This was yesterday? You were back at the mall."

"Nostalgia." The mall was, after all, where we met. At the far border of the food court, where people spin by like wind at world's edge.

"And you did it again. You walked up to someone you don't know and told them this horrible thing was going to happen to them. You told me you stopped doing that."

"I had."

Becca sips her coffee disgruntledly. Not many could pull that off. The word *aplomb* falls into my mind.

"How many times have we talked about this? In what alternate universe did you think it was a good idea? What could you possibly hope to accomplish? What has it *ever* accomplished?"

I remain silent. Becca's questions are like the lyrics of an old song that always takes you back to adolescence, to your first heartbreak when moon and sun shut down, to that third or fourth date when you just knew. I'm listening to them, running them, in my mind.

"It's one thing to dwell on horrible things, Ken. Polish wedding chairs, bed bug infestations, holes in the space-time continuum. It's quite another to tell people these awful things are going to happen."

"They're true."

"Your telling about them is not going to matter. They will still happen. All you've done is make someone horribly sad."

"I can't help myself."

"Of course you can."

"Just say no?"

"Just keep your mouth shut."

Which is what I decide to do, even though there's so much I have to tell her. That I was at the mall for good reason, for the comfort of memories. Or about her new dress, how good she looks in it. How this is the only time she'll wear it. How it's the one she'll be buried in.

Billy Deliver's Next Twelve Novels

The dogs took him down a few miles outside Topeka.

⟋

When he came to from a forty-year coma, his favorite show from back when he was a kid was on the TV hung by two struts from the ceiling. *Space Rangers*. The screws of one strut had pulled partially loose. Threads were visible; the whole structure canted starboard.

⟋

It's always a kick to go visit Berr. He's got these cardboard cutouts of his parents and sister that he moves around the house, from bed to bathroom to breakfast table to living room. Tonight we're sitting at the table with them finishing off a ten-dollar pizza.

I've not spoken to the person who lives in my garage. She slipped in there one evening a month or so back when, in a hurry to get to work and already late, I failed to close the automatic door.

⁄

Just now I walked up to the office and asked where this was. Nothing in the room offered a clue: no information sheets, emergency card, notepad, old newspaper. No relevant signs outside, a service station across the street down a block or so with ancient pumps that look like gumball machines. The sign painted on the office window says *Motel*. The guy who came out of the back had skin flaking like the paint on the sign.

⁄

He'd just bought a box of memories marked down half-price at GoMart and settled in to enjoy them when the phone rang. He froze the DreamBox on a slow-moving tropical beach complete with seagulls the size of mastiffs and punched in the phone.

⁄

The day we sold Dad for parts, we celebrated by going out for a big breakfast at Griddles, the place we met 25 years ago. Damn miracle it still existed. Damn miracle that we did too, of course—as a pair, I mean.

She smells the smoke on me and senses, beyond that, subtler betrayals. She doesn't say anything, though, just hands me the glass of wine she's already poured, one she says has legs, not balls mind you, but legs.

⁂

The toaster said "No."
  "Why not?"
  "That's not how you like it. Buttered, lightly toasted."
  "I long to try something new. Take the plunge. Live wild."
  "You won't like it."
  That's how the day began.

⁂

One bright morning Charlie fired up his computer to find himself, much to his surprise, for sale on Ebay. The bids were appallingly low.

⁂

The alien sat in the bare room across from him. It looked exactly like Sanderson's fifth-grade teacher. Somehow a fly had got in the room. Sanderson noted that the fly avoided the part of the room where the alien was.

⁂

In the last moments, they say, William Blake jumped up from his death bed and began to sing.

Figs

Light spills out cracks of beer joint walls tonight as I patrol. Past eleven and the town's quiet. In another two hours those beer joints themselves will spill into the streets. Down by the town square where, beneath the old bandstand, feral cats bring weekly generations of kittens into the world, imperfectly cleared leavings from today's farmer's market glitter in the streetlights. Seven hours from now they'll be setting up again. I'd have to remember to check with Dominic tomorrow. Should be just about time for the good ones, and he always has the best.

There's nothing I love more than driving the streets of town at night. A single light shows through curtains at the pastor's home behind Savior Methodist. Sal's OneStop is still open, as is his front door, with country music streaming out from inside. Half a mile past the city limits a familiar truck sits empty at roadside, keys in the ignition. Nate Brown drunk again no doubt and, suddenly gone aware he shouldn't be driving, taken to foot for the remaining distance, as happens once or twice a week.

Swinging back into town proper, I come across a couple of high schoolers, faces familiar, names unknown, with a stalled-out Camry. The car has what look to be freehand swirls, vaguely winglike, along the sides. The car's seen some wear. They haven't, not much, not yet. The boy peeks out from under the hood as he hears me pull up. She gets out of the driver's seat and they walk back together to meet me. Turns out it's only a bad battery connection. They're back on the road in minutes, probably on their way out to Blue Hole, the lake everyone around here claims is bottomless, a favored spot for what we called parking when I was a kid.

When I was five or six, I fell out of a fig tree. Yeah, you gotta be small to do that, and I was. My parents had a bunch of these, a grape arbor, tulips. At the time I had no idea how exotic all this was, for where we lived. I remember being on my back on the ground, trying to breathe and not being able to, getting up and stumbling toward the house, and my mother running to me—then suddenly the pressure gave way and my chest filled. Tears ran down both our cheeks.

There's rain in the offing, you see it in the halos around lights but can't feel or taste it just yet. By early morning, maybe. Be a mess for the farmer's market.

My last touchstone on the way back into town, as always, is the old Merritt place, abandoned years ago upon Ezra's death at 82 and his wife's the following week (from heartbreak as they say), now suspended ownerless in real-estate purgatory but kept up sporadically, lawn mowed, porch and frontage hosed down, by neighbors. It reminds me how things once were.

Back at the office there's a logged call from a number I don't recognize. Billie's confined to bed by doctor's orders for the next two months before her third child's due, and Marty's filling in for her at dispatch. We call it dispatch even though it's more like answer the phone, make sure the doors are locked, keep the coffee fresh. Nope, wouldn't leave a name, Marty says when I ask, and when I call, twice, there's no answer. Then ten minutes later we get a call that gives us an address after saying "Something's going on over there." Marty checks. The address corresponds to the number that called earlier.

There's no answer at the door, no one in the house when I go in, no sign of disturbance. According to records, a Mabel Clark lives here, possibly with a teenage son. Out in the kitchen, dishes and utensils, a pot and small skillet, are in the draining rack over the left sink. There's milk a week away from expiration in the refrigerator, a pack of ham slices gone slimy, multiple plastic buckets of leftovers, a loaf of brown bread you could use as a door stop. Beds in both bedrooms aren't made but have covers and sheets pulled to the top and folded back. The alarm clock's preset to 6:50 AM.

I don't have to wake Mrs. Sim, the neighbor who called it in. She's waiting for me on her front porch and wants to know if everything's okay but has nothing to add to what she said before on the phone: Heard what she first thought was loud TV then thought maybe could be shouts, and they didn't stop, just went on and on until, all of a sudden, there was some kind of crash and it all stopped, which is when she called.

I thank her and go back over for one last look. No evidence of anything crashing, getting thrown, broken. Mrs. Sim told me where Mabel Clark works and I'll check there first thing in the morning. No other kin she's aware of, except Rich, her son, but he hasn't been around for months, far as she knows.

Rain's getting a little closer, a little bolder, as I get back to the truck. A mockingbird in the tree I'm parked under thinks it's still daytime and busily tries out all four parts of a vocal quartet one after another.

Figs were one of the first plants to be cultivated by humans before going on to wheat, barley or legumes. The beginning of agriculture, really. Aristotle noted that there were two kinds, the cultivated fig that bears fruit, the wild fig that assists the first. Buddha's enlightenment came beneath the Bodhi Tree, a sacred fig (*Ficus religiosa*) with heart-shaped leaves.

Things are quiet for a while. I draft a report on the call about Mabel Clark in longhand and, while I'm entering it, pull up her workplace on the computer, an auto parts store next town over, then go poking about for son Rich as well. No results. From what I hear about social media, he's probably on there somewhere, but for me that's undiscovered country, another world.

Marty brings in two cups of coffee from a fresh pot he just made and we sit talking. I hear faint crackles out front from the ham radio receiver he brings to work with him. He offers a portion from a homemade cookie the size of a dinner plate, but I decline. He tells me about a new woman he's dating, someone he met at the community college where he's taking Spanish classes. Her grandparents were from Mexico, but she never learned.

Along about two, the hospital calls, the new doctor from out of state, to tell me Danny brought in a DOA in the ambulance and I'm needed. When I ask who it is, she says Evelyn Crawford, do I know her? My English teacher in tenth grade.

Evelyn likes her television, Otis tells me when I get there, and he doesn't have much patience for silly stories, so he goes on about his business at the table out in the den while she watches at night. She always mutes the commercials when they come on. But a couple hours ago he noticed the thing was still going full volume, with someone talking about laundry soap or the last flashlight you'll ever need. Thinking back, he realized it had been that way for a while, and when he went in to see, he found Evelyn dead in her chair.

Looks like heart failure, the new doctor says. She's considerably older than I'd have thought from her voice on the phone, slow-talking, quiet-spoken. Nothing suspicious here then, I ask. Just notifying you as required, she tells me. Good to meet you, by the way.

A year after Jean and I got married, two stupid wide-eyed kids ready to take on the world, we moved to New York. Brooklyn really, an Italian neighborhood with women forever out on the front stoop and men playing dominoes at card tables on the sidewalk. The apartment we rented was upstairs of a restaurant, big burly guys in there all day long sitting at tables drinking, shirts half unbuttoned with hair spilling out, gold chains. The owner's ancient mother lived upstairs too. Jean said she never felt safer in her life, nobody in his right mind would come near the place. One morning I went down to pay the rent and the owner was eating fresh figs, selectively plucking them out of a basket with two fingers like people do candies from a box. You like figs? the owner asked, seeing my interest. I told him about our trees, when I was a kid. An hour later there came a knock at the apartment door and one of the big guys stood there with a basket of figs.

I'm barely out of the hospital parking lot when Marty radios to let me know the alarm's going off at Hobb's Hardware again. This happens five, six times a month. Anything can serve to set it off, high wind, sudden noises, heavy trucks rolling too close by. I've repeatedly asked, less and less pleasantly, that Karl have the alarm company out to fix this, and he always says he will. It's got so bad I have a key to the place.

Nothing to see from outside when I get there, front or rear. I give it time to let my eyes adjust better to darkness, then let myself in the front door. Shadowy light from the streetlamp outside falls through the front windows but gives up quickly. Ten or twelve steps from the door, everything's black as a cave. I go in slowly, one footstep then another, listening between.

For a moment I think I see a flash of light at the back of the store, by the warehouse, and that I hear something scrabbling—a large rat, maybe. Here in the oldest parts of town, with bins of trash in the alleys, the cockroaches and general decay, rats can grow to rabbit size. A pickup goes by outside, its lights sweeping the back wall. In the bare seconds they last, again I think I see something back there, movement maybe.

I'm almost to the back of the store myself now.

When I found Jean's body, I stood at the bedroom door for what seemed a very long time. With all the blood, there was no question but that she was dead and, from the blood's appearance, little doubt that she'd been so for hours before I came home from a quiet night on patrol. Beside her on the nightstand, half eaten, was the carton of figs I'd left for her on the kitchen table, an anniversary gift, complete with card that read *Remember?*

Sunday Drive

Because it's the weekend, traffic is light, and once we get out of downtown, where I parked on the street quite a ways off, having made the parking-lot mistake once before, we've got smooth sailing, calm seas, all that. Caroline stares out the window, talking about how much this area has changed, the whole city, really, that you can hardly recognize it from what it used to be. Mattie, in the back, is texting one-handed on her new iPhone, nibbling at a Pop-Tart in such a way that the edge is always even. She holds it away from her mouth every few bites to check.

When I suggest that we take a little drive, not hurry home, Mattie groans, then looks away as I glance in the rear view mirror. "Whatever you want is fine," Caroline says.

I jump on I-10, then the 202 out toward Tempe and all those other far-flung lands. Back years ago, when Caroline and I were first married, I worked these roads, running heavy equipment, backhoes, bulldozers. Knew every mile of highway, every block of city street. Then I went back to school and got my degree. Now I program computers and solve IT problems all day long. Now I can barely find my way around out here in this world.

"The music was lovely," Caroline says. "Back there."

"Puccini, yes."

"The story was dumb," Mattie says, leaning hard on the final word. So at least she was paying that much attention.

We drive out past the airport and hotels to the left, cheap apartments, garages and ramshackle convenience stores to the right, past a building that looks like a battleship and that I swear was not here the last time we came this way, past the two hills near the zoo that look like humongous dung heaps. Wind is picking up, blowing food wrappers and blossoms from bougainvillea in bursts across the road.

Caroline fidgets with the radio, cakewalking through top forty, light jazz, classical, country. Trying to regain something of what we felt momentarily, by proxy, back there? Trying to muffle the silence that presses down on us? Or just bored? What the hell do *I* know about human motivation, anyway?

On impulse I exit, loop around, and get on the 51 heading north. Soon we're cruising through the stretch of cactus-spackled hills everyone calls Dreamy Draw. Caroline has something peppy and lilting about a lost love playing on the radio. Ukulele is involved. Mattie leans forward to listen to the music as three Harleys come up on our left, their throaty *raaaa* like a bubble enclosing us. All three riders have expensive leather jackets and perfectly cut hair.

At the 101, the Harleys swing right towards Scottsdale. We head west for I-17 to begin the slow climb out of the valley, through Deadman Wash, Bumble Bee, Rock Springs. Where clouds hang above hills, the hills are dark. Nascent yellow blooms sprout from the ends of saguaro arms. Caroline stares off, not towards the horizon or into green-shot gorges, but out her window at dry flatland and cholla. Mattie is asleep.

In the distance, out over one of the mesas, hawks glide on thermals.

△

Hard on to the end of the second act of *Turandot*, about the time Calif was getting ready to ring the gong and lay his life on the line for love, the old geezer sitting in front of me, the one whose wife had been elbowing him to keep awake, began weeping uncontrollably. She elbowed him again, more English on it this time, and after a moment he struggled to his feet and staggered up the stairs and out. I followed. When I caught up, he was standing motionless by one of the windows. He could have been part of a diorama, 21st century man in his unnatural habitat.

"You okay?"

He looked up, looked at the window, finally looked at me. I could see the world struggling to reboot behind his eyes.

A minute ago I was thinking how all these people paid sixty or a hundred dollars to spiff themselves up and sit through two hours of largeness and artifice—grand emotion, bright colors, carnival—before going back to their own small lives. Now I was thinking about just one of those people, and how sometimes we find expression for our pain, how it can just fall upon us.

"I didn't want to come to this. My wife's employer, she works for a doctor, he gave her tickets he couldn't use. She insisted we come. I knew it was a bad idea."

"Because . . . ?"

He shook his head.

"Let's get some air," I said.

We stepped outside, where life-size sculptures of dancers, canted forward on one leg, arms outstretched, had found refuge from time and the earth's pull. A beautiful day. Across the street an old woman stood behind a cardboard podium singing arias much like those going on inside. Poorly dyed gray hair fell in strands that looked like licorice sticks. Her dress had once been purple. My companion was watching her, no expression on his face.

He took out his wallet, pulled something from one of the photo holders and began unfolding it.

"Nineteen seventy-six, when I was working the pipeline." He held it out for me to see. "Twelve hundred and ninety dollars. One week's work."

It was a check. You could make that out, but not much else. When I looked back up and smiled, he looked at the check.

"Guess you can't make it out too good anymore."

He folded it carefully, put it back. Glanced again at the diva, who had one foot in the door of *Nessun dorma*. The strangeness of hearing the piece as a soprano aria matched perfectly the strangeness of the setting.

"Well, young man," he said, "we should go back in now."

We did, and even before I retook my seat I sensed that something had changed. The audience seemed poised, expectant. And was there a void onstage? One of several court scenes, better than a dozen attendants and functionaries in place. The patterns were wrong. What, I asked, sliding in next to Caroline, had happened?

A cast member, the forester she thought, had collapsed and been spirited out, with barely a breath's hesitation, by two others.

Made quite a rattle and bang when he hit the floor. It was a major aria for the ice princess, of course, and with but a moment's glance toward the commotion, the soprano had flawlessly continued, inching toward the inevitable high C or whatever it was. A woman two rows back had asked her companions, loudly, if this was a part of the show.

The rest passed without incident, building inexorably to its grandly happy, unrelenting conclusion, soprano soaring like a seabird, tenor stolidly tossing his voice to the rafters, chorus dug in and determined to hold its own, orchestra a-clash with horns and percussion.

Turandot had been wrong.

Now the riddles were solved, the gong would sound no more.

And we were outside, moving within moving corridors of other opera-goers, past the bronze dancers, past the diva with her cardboard podium, reclaimed by our lives.

◁

Just this side of Sunset Point, Mattie has one of her seizures. Doesn't happen much anymore, with the medication, but we're used to it from the old days. Something starts thumping against the seat, I look back, and it's her legs spasming. I edge off the road, get in the back with her, and hold her till it stops. From the first, right after Mattie was born, Caroline never was much good at handling that. She'd fall to pieces or just kind of go away. As the seizures got worse, so did the going away. I don't blame her. Or anyone. Things just happen.

We're back on the road in four, five minutes, Caroline looking out the window, Mattie sleeping it off. We inch up the hill and around a long curve behind three semis. Our speed drops to 55, 48, 44, 40. Atop the hill we're able to pass. I roll down the window. The air is fresh and cool. Something with that unmistakable pulse of baroque music, strings, horns, keyboard continuo, plays on the radio. It begins to cut out, like a stutterer, as we gain altitude.

Mattie wakes, rattles a box of Jolly Ranchers to see how much is left, pops one in her mouth and sucks away. We're ten thousand feet up and there's a pinpoint puncture, our air's hissing slowly out. That's what it sounds like.

"What do you want to do about dinner?" Caroline says.

I'm thinking about a movie I'd like to see. There's this family. The father goes off to his job every day, it's exciting work, all about people and solving real problems for them, and he comes home and talks about it over the dinner table, where they all eat together. The mother's a teacher, so she tells what went on at school, funny things her kids said today, how much better some of them are doing, how others still have problems with fractions or irregular verbs or something like that. The daughter talks about school too, and her friends, and about track-team practice this afternoon. She's healthy, vibrant, and isn't going to die before she ever gets to be an adult.

"We can pick up burgers at the corner on the way home," Caroline says. "That work for you?"

I think of Montezuma's Castle just miles from here, an entire city built high into a hillside, accessible only by long ladders. Back in the day we'd go on picnics at a little park not far from there. I want to say, "There's no magic left in my name, little one. No magic anymore in these hills. In the sun, yes, and in the sky. But those are far away." I don't, of course.

We're into the thick of it now, hill and curve, hill and curve. The drop offs have shifted to the right, Caroline's side. In a minute we'll be there, the highest point, the deepest drop. I pick up speed and Caroline looks over at me. Upset that I'm going too fast? Or does she sense something more?

I look in the rear view mirror. Mattie has gone back to sleep. Good.

This is where we get off.

The World Is the Case

Tucked beneath my feet as I glide into the long, banking curve is the briefcase, one foot in sensible shoe resting atop it. The city sits like a saddle in the sudden hollow of mountains. You come through a pass and it springs into being there below. Each time you feel as settlers must have felt. I duck my head to peer over the rim of sunglasses at the rear view mirror. I can't see them, but I know the others are back there.

There's the usual run of gas stations, quick stops and antique or junk shops on the outskirts, a lumberyard, three or four confusing signs with lists of highways and state roads. A building that's half family café, half biker bar, whose pies are, as it says right there on the front window, world famous.

The car bumps as it passes over the remains of a squashed cat, raccoon or skunk. The briefcase under my foot doesn't budge. The radio brings in distraction and disaster from a larger world, news that has nothing to do with this place, this moment in time, why I am here. Clouds nudge at sky's edge, blind and feeling their way.

The briefcase, too, is from another world. Fine leather, roughly the size and shape of an old-time doctor's bag, with a hinged top closing onto a smaller section that tucks perfectly beneath the seat, as though car and case were made for one another.

All my life I'd waited for my ship to come in but, near as I could tell, the thing never left port. Instead I was steadily going down, the way they say Venice is sinking into the sea. Dive, dive, dive. Until I found the briefcase.

By then I wasn't on my uppers, I was living on the *memory* of my uppers, hanging out in bus stations, libraries and parks, sleeping where I could, scavenging alleyways behind restaurants for food. Jackson Park's a favorite, high-traffic so as not to stand out so much, midtown and close to the financial district so as to make for good, guilt-driven panhandles, and that's where I was, leaning against one tree in the shadow of another, when a young man (fashionable three-day growth of beard, diamond stud left ear) in an old suit (narrow lapels, pegged trousers) walked past, came back, and sat on the bench before me. The bench had a four-color advertisement for Motivational Yoga on it. The young man had a thoughtful smile.

He tucked the briefcase beneath the bench and looked off into the trees where strands of bird song—warnings, come-hithers, idle chatter—wove themselves into thatch. After a moment he rose, leaving the briefcase behind. And yes, I thought to call after him. Thought to search out some official to whom I might turn it over. But did neither. Instead went back to my tree and waited with it on the ground by me, in the same shadow as myself.

Maybe some things are meant to be, you know?

Once I found the briefcase, I began to find other things. Money, in a suitcase from a dumpster behind Durant's. Emerald cufflinks and jewelry in the purse of a woman who shared my seat on the light rail and bounded off at the last moment as doors closed.

This car.

I pull into the next souvenir shop I come to, thinking about what's inside: decorative shot glasses, pepper jelly, books of jokes and local history, hot sauce, spoon rests and ashtrays in the shape of cowboy gear, Indian jewelry. I look across the highway at brown, bare hills, scrub cholla and saguaro cactus as cars behind me pass, cars I have been tracking.

The desert is honest; it makes no promises. Is this why I've come here?

The dark gray Buick pulls into a quick stop just up the road. A middle-aged man gets out the passenger side but doesn't stray. He walks the car's perimeter, makes to be checking tires. Like the man who left the briefcase back in the park he wears an old-fashioned suit. Skinny lapels, pant legs echoing their taper. I go inside, purchase an ice cream sandwich and linger eating it, standing by the car. The man up the way goes around front to raise the hood.

I pull back onto the road. Two or three minutes pass before the Buick floats up in my rear view mirror. There are few enough cut-offs that it can stay far back.

I reach down and run my fingers across the top of the case, soft and smooth as skin. My thumb rests on the monogram, brass like the hasps, hinges and feet, before moving to the lock. Even here, pushing ninety degrees outside, the lock is cold to the touch.

I have never opened the briefcase. And never will now, whatever happens, whatever comes next. It has done its work.

◻

Zombie Cars
A film by James Sallis

Turn the clocks forward eighty years.

Oil resources are depleted, the cities have emptied, much of America has returned to rural living. Rumors begin to circulate, then "unconfirmed reports" by media: old cars and trucks are rising up from the ground and from wrecking yards like zombies of old, losing parts and drooling fluids as they move toward centers of population seeking gasoline and oil.

Little is remembered of the ancient technology.

But outside Iowa City, where the Amish have grown affluent producing buggies for the entire country, one boy knows about the old vehicles. Ridiculed as "car crazy" by peers, an exasperation to his single mother, he is obsessed with automobiles and the culture they engendered, his room filled to bursting with photos of classic cars, drive-in restaurants, filling stations and racetracks, his shelves sparsely but lovingly stacked with copies of Hot Rod Magazine and ancient books hunted down and purchased with the money he makes as an apprentice farrier.

Finally the reports can no longer be denied. The revenant vehicles are everywhere, lurching toward Bethlehem, Des Moines, Keokuk, and Cedar Rapids.

"Yet again the wretched excesses of our past come back to plague us," a politician says on an election swing through St. Louis.

"Who would have thought undeath had done so many," a poet intones at a rally near Gary, Indiana.

"We must reach down, down deep, to find the carburetor and differential within us," a lay preacher implores from a Wisconsin pulpit.

And in a farmhouse outside Iowa City, the one person who just *knows* he can help, has to make the decision of his life: to go against his mother's explicit orders, or to save mankind.

Meanwhile, among the revenants, factions develop, some crusading to wipe out the humans to whom they owe their existence, others to accommodate and co-exist. My personal favorite scene is a revival meeting held in the ruins of a drive-in theatre, a Ford F-150 truck preaching to a field of vehicles who hear his sermon and entreaties both through the malfunctioning speakers on stands and through the cracked speakers of their own radios. (Throughout, the vehicles speak with sound: motors, creaks, horns. Translations appear as subtitles.)

Another pivotal scene has Tim sitting in his room reading. He is listening to news about the zombie cars on a crystal radio he's built into an ancient plastic model Thunderbird; from time to time he turns off the volume to hear, in the distance, the rumble of vehicles reviving and extricating themselves from the wrecking yard miles away. He is reading the end of *Gulliver's Travels*, where Gulliver, after his time with the Houyhnhms, has become a misfit amongst his own, passing his time chatting with horses in the stables.

Finally, Tim makes his decision, leaves a note for his mother, and strikes out, with a change of underwear, a Popular Mechanics guide and mechanic's tools bundled into a bag at the end of a stick, as he's seen in pictures of hobos.

He *knows* he can help. No doubt about it, none at all. Just isn't sure how.

Following a number of encounters with humans and revenant vehicles, he almost becomes collateral damage in a zombie-human stand-off but is rescued by a renegade zombie, a psychedelic-painted VW van. The van once belonged ("for a long, long time—if, of course, you believe in time") to a philosopher, and has learned to communicate through its radio speaker.

Together Tim and the van, who Tim decides has to be named Gogh, find their way through battling humans and revenants, lone wolf vigilante humans, and splinter groups including a small troop of revenant vehicles repeatedly "killing" themselves for the greater good, only to be again reborn. Eventually Tim and van Gogh encounter and join others like themselves, humans and vehicles who have formed alliances.

The way of the future, they all begin to understand, will not be one or the other, soft machine, hard machine, living, unliving—but both.

"We're not locked into Aristotelian logic like you," van Gogh explains to Tim in one of his frequent philosophical musings, "we're not locked into logic at all. It's not *either/or*, Tim. It's all one big *and*. Always has been."

A shrewd critic* has written that in science fiction two endings are possible: either you blow up the world, or things go back to how they were before. Ever the team for challenge, for going that extra inch or two, and for utterly ignoring the

reasonable, we figured out a way to do both—so don't miss
Zombie Cars when it comes clanking and leaking to a theater
near you.

∏

* me

Net Loss

What happened was, the TV in the next room heard my girlfriend and me arguing and called the police. Those thunks they heard were me slamming the refrigerator door then, later, dropping my coffee cup and bagel plate. But you ever tried to explain a thing like that, when they just keep playing the recording again and again and won't let you pee?

Did you know your TV could do that?

One of the cops that showed up at the door had spent years being a lot heavier. Loose skin swayed under his arms, he walked with splayed feet, his shirt was a couple sizes too big. Made you wonder whether he'd been overweight and was working on it or was just on his way out of this world. The other seemed headed in the opposite direction, gaining girth and stature as the first one shrank. The bigger guy also seemed to be lead, with little guy holding down harmony parts.

At the arraignment my court-appointed lawyer reminded them they couldn't call the TV as a witness and they all had a big yuck over that. Smoothing her skirt that looked like a test pattern, she rolled out a string of letters and numbers and so on that were supposed to be law code but I'm pretty sure were just made up. Twice, she made me pull out my earbuds. Third time, she reached up and yanked them out herself—and right out of the phone. I was listening to the Blind Boys of Alabama. You ever heard them? Sweet. "Mother's Children Have a Hard Time," "God Knows Everything."

Figure that jail's as close to army living as I'm ever gonna get. All of us packed up in there like chickens with nowhere to go and nothing to do but peck at each other over every damn thing. "Hmmm. Patchouli, BO, tasty testosterone, old whiskey, a hint of the fecal—yum!" as Sweet William said. Then there was Reader. And the guy who tried giving him grief, who wasn't with us long. Afterwards, Reader took his finger out from between pages and went back to his book. No matter how many times they got corrected, Sweet Willie and Crusher kept on calling our new homes holding cells. "Everybody wants to get held, am I right?"

I spent two weeks in such fine company. When they let me out I walked what has to be two, three miles back to the apartment and found it empty. My clothes and stuff, my turntable rig and my collection of old vinyl were there. The rest was gone. Carla'd left a note saying if that's the kind of man I was, I was going to have to be it without her.

I'll be straight with you, I was glad as sunshine she took that damn TV.

My player got taken away from me at the jail and when they gave me back my billfold and keys and stuff, it wasn't there. Not on the intake list, they told me, sorry, no sign of it. So the first thing I had to do was go out and get a new one from the big box store. Picked up some Blind Boys and other tunes while I was there—paid for those. When I got back, there was a note slid under my door from the apartment manager saying that since I was of questionable moral standing and two months behind in rent, I should be out of the apartment and off the property by the end of the week. I went down to his apartment, pushed the door open—none of them had locks that worked worth a shit—and spoke with him concerning this. He'd heard about the cops, he told me. Went to the city website, saw the assault charges against me, talked to Carla as she was loading up the U-Haul. Then he got this flagged email from a group called WatchUp.

So now I learn I'm on this posting list that gets circulated to warn everyone about sex offenders, murderers, parolees, and people like me moving into their neighborhood. While I was there, since Carla took hers, I borrowed the manager's computer to check on the website. They had an old photo of me up. Not sure anyone would recognize me from it, I don't look much like that anymore. It was from, what, six or eight years ago? Life, not to mention jail, had changed me.

But it's like finally I know who I am, what my life's about. I look at the manager duct-taped to the chair and go out to the kitchen to find the right tool for the job. While I'm raking through drawers—no lawyer to snatch them out, here—I punch in my earbuds, hit play, and the Blind Boys start up singing, "Almost Home." I think how my old man was always saying TV's bad for you. Guess he was right about that. And I'm thinking how when the time comes, long after they take my music away, the Blind Boys will still be singing, on and on, and how I'll go down with their songs, with all this beauty, in my heart.

⁊

Season Premiere

It was just after they hung Shorty Bergen that the rats showed up.

No one had ever seen anything like them. They came swarming up over the bank of a dried-up riverbed, must have been close to a hundred of them, traveling all together. It was like locusts in those films of Africa, where the bugs sweep down and leave behind nothing but bare branches and stalks. Only the rats weren't looking for vegetable matter. Johnny Jones lost his whole crop of chickens. At Gene Brocato's they took down five sheep and a young cow.

"Rats don't hunt in packs," Billy Barnstile said. He and his partner Joe McGee were out in one of the power company's trucks, checking lines. They'd pulled off the road to watch as the rats broke into twin streams around the farmhouse then rejoined to sweep over Gene Brocato's field. Within moments, it seemed, only bones remained where livestock had been.

"Never saw anything like it," Joe McGee said.

Of course, no one had ever seen anything like Shorty Bergen either. He looked like parts of two people glued together, this long, long trunk with a couple of stubby doll legs stuck on as afterthought. "Boy'd had legs to match his body, he'd be eight feet tall," his mother always said. But he wasn't. He was four-and-a-half feet tall, even in the goat-roper cowboy boots he favored. Hair stuck out in bristles from his ears. His real hair, however often he washed it, always looked greasy, all two dozen or so limp strands of it.

What had happened was, Shorty'd taken himself a liking to Betty Sue Carstairs, and there was two things wrong with that. Dan Carstairs was nearabout the only person in town with anything like real money, and he loved his daughter, who'd come to him late in life, with a fierce pride—that's one—and Betty Sue, for all her beauty—this is two—was simple as a fence post. When Shorty Bergen started bringing her candy and bundles of wildflowers he'd picked on the way through the woods, she babbled and drooled in delight. Didn't have no idea how ugly he was, or that anything might be wrong in it, or what he was up to. Her daddy'd always brought her things. Now Shorty did too.

Pretty soon the rats were all the talk down at Bee's Blue Bell Diner, which, if you didn't eat at home, was where you ate in Hank's Ridge.

"They ain't come near town as yet, at least," Lucas Hodgkins said. Some egg yolk and about a third of his upper dentures had slipped his mouth. He reached up and pushed the dentures back in. The egg yolk stayed.

"I hear you." This was Froggie Levereaux, four tables away. People said he ordered that damned beret he always wore from Sears. He sure as hell hadn't bought it in Hank's Ridge. His nose put you in mind of the blade on a sundial. "You never know, though. Onct they get a taste of human blood . . . I seen it happen with huntin' dogs. Even with a goat, one time. Commenced to gobbling up small children like popcorn."

Bee, herself, a dry stick of a woman, was in the thick of it.

"Don't like it, don't like it at all," she said. Bee hadn't liked much of anything in well onto forty-six years.

"Where've they been is what I want to know. None of us ever heard tell of 'em."

"I remember when I was little, back in Florida, it used to rain frogs."

"Frogs is frogs. Rats is rats."

"It's like that story about the paid piper."

"Boils be next," Judd Sealey said, a deacon down to the church, "boils. Then—well, I can't rightly remember. Seven of them, though. Seven plagues."

"Rodents, is what they are." Bud Gooley shuddered. "Teeth don't never stop growing."

The sound of the screen door out to the kitchen swinging shut brought a hiatus to the conversation.

Jed Stanton shook his head sagely. "You ever know Stu Ellum to leave behind a perfectly good bite of pie before?"

Froggie Levereaux ambled over and finished it up for him.

"Man's got him a worry for sure," Bee said.

Dan Carstairs warned Shorty Bergen to stay away from Betty Sue and went into some detail as to what would eventuate if he failed to do so. Thing was, taken as he was with Betty Sue, Shorty Bergen had gone damn near as simple as the girl herself. He'd just stand there smiling up at Dan Carstairs. Nobody laid claim to having seen it, but everyone knew how one Saturday evening when Shorty Bergen came courting, Dan Carstairs proceeded to have his farmhands stretch Shorty out against an old wagon wheel and went at him with a bullwhip, dousing him with salted water afterwards. Shorty Bergen never said a word, never once whimpered or cried out. Next day, there he was as usual, with flowers and candy for Miss Betty Sue.

Stuart Ellum lived two or three miles south of town on what had once been a thriving apple orchard. Years back some unknown disease had attacked the trees, moving from limb to limb, turning apples into lines of tiny shrunken heads. Limbs twisted and deformed, trunks bloated, the trees remained.

Stu Ellum also had a daughter, Sylvie. The two of them lived in a shack overgrown with honeysuckle and patched with old tin signs for soft drinks. There'd been a wife too for a while, but no one knew much about her, or just when it was she left, if leave she did. A hill woman, they said. Some of the old women used to avert their eyes whenever she came around.

Sylvie never showed any interest in going into town the way Stuart did a couple of times a week, or really in leaving the place at all. She cooked, cleaned their clothes in the stream nearby. Other than that she'd sit on a rickety chair outside the cabin watching bees, wasps and hummingbirds have at the honeysuckle, or head off into the woods and be gone for hours at a time.

Then a while back, in one of the hollows where people hereabouts are wont to dump garbage, she'd come across a TV set and hauled it back to the cabin. Its innards were all gone, but the glass in front was still good. Sylvie put it up on an old crate in one corner of the cabin and commenced to carve little tables and beds and chairs and buildings. She'd set these up inside, then go across the room and sit watching. One day when Stuart Ellum walked in, he saw she had insects, a grasshopper, a katydid, sitting at the little table inside the TV, acting out whatever scene Sylvie had in her mind.

Over the next several weeks, Shorty Bergen had got himself horsewhipped a second time, beat with axe handles till three ribs broke, and thrown in the pen, hobbled, with one of Dan Carstairs' famously mean-tempered goats. Each time he popped right back up. Carstairs would head out to check on the ploughing or to buy feed and come back and there that boy'd be, sitting on the porch holding hands with Betty Sue.

Must have been right about then that Dan Carstairs decided on taking a different tack.

He started putting it out that Shorty Bergen had raped his Betty Sue. She wasn't the first either, by his reckoning, he said, and men folk all 'round the valley had best look to their wives and daughters.

Probably nothing would've come of it, except a couple families over the other side of the mountain started saying somebody'd been getting to their girls too. Never mind that just about everybody knew exactly who it was had been getting to them. That kind of thing, once it starts up, it spreads like wildfire. Wasn't more than a month had passed before Shorty Bergen woke to a flashlight in his eyes and a group of stern-faced men above him. They dragged him outside, tied a rope around his neck in a simple granny knot and threw the rope over a limb, and a bunch of them hauled at the other end. When the limb broke, they started over, and got the job done, though it took some time.

Now, it happened that Sylvie had taken a liking to Shorty Bergen. One of the ways he scraped together a living was by scavenging what people threw away, everything from chairs to simple appliances, and fixing them. Then he'd take them around and sell them for a dollar or two. He'd only been by Stuart Ellum's cabin twice, since Stuart always told him they had everything they needed and then some, but Sylvie never took her eyes off him either time, and afterwards was always asking Stuart about him. Before that, whenever she told Stuart about her shows, they were full of doctors and nurses, rich men who lived alone in great sadness, and young women suddenly come upon unsuspected legacies or gifts, like all those soap operas she'd seen on a visit to her aunt in the city. Once she saw Shorty Bergen, though, all her shows centered around him. Shorty was running for sheriff but the rich man who owned everything hereabouts was bound and determined to see him defeated. The doctors at the hospital had done something to Shorty at birth. A withered Native American shook a child's rattle of feathers over his still body and warned that if Shorty were to die, his spirit would sweep like a storm across the land, cleansing it, purifying it.

"Girl? Girl?" What have you done?" Stuart Ellum asked as he ducked to enter the cabin. All the way back from the diner he'd been thinking about what he'd heard there, about that pack of rats overrunning everything, sheep and cattle going down beneath them, a flood of rats laying waste to everything in its path.

"Shhh, it's the news," Sylvie said.

Behind the glass of the TV two rats sat upright in tiny chairs looking straight out into the room. They took turns talking, glancing down at the table before them from time to time, other times looking at one another with knowing nods.

Soon Sylvie clapped her hands silently and turned towards him.

"What did you want to ask me, Daddy?"

As she turned towards him, so did the two rats sitting at the little table inside the TV. Then they stood and took a bow. Their eyes shone—the rats' eyes, and his daughter's.

⫽

As Yet Untitled

I am to be, they tell me, in a new Western series, so I've tried on a shirt with snaps for buttons and a hat the size of a chamber pot and stood for hours before the mirror practicing the three S's: slouch, sidle, and squint. It's been a good life these past years inhabiting the science fiction novels of Iain Shore, but science fiction sales are falling, they tell me, plummeting in fact, so they've decided to get ahead of the curve and move me along. Back to mysteries? I ask, with fond memories of fedoras, smoke-filled rooms, the bite of cheap whiskey. Sales there are even worse, they tell me, and hand across my new clothes. Howdy, my new editor says.

Next day I meet my author, who definitely ain't no Iain Shore. (At least I'm getting the lingo down.) Evidently, from the look of his unwashed hair, what's left of it, he doesn't believe in tampering with what nature's given him. His lips hang half off his face like huge water blisters there below rheumy red eyes. He's wearing a sport coat that puts me in mind of shrink-wrapping, trousers that look like the gray workpants sold at Sears, and a purplish T-shirt doing valiant duty against his pudge.

By way of acknowledgment, he pushes his glasses up his nose. They're back down before his hand is.

"Woodrow," he says. My name, evidently.

His is Evan, which he pronounces (my editor tells me) *Even*.

"I've the bulk of the thing worked out," Evan says. "All but the end, I should say. And the title—I don't have my title yet. First title, I mean. Not to worry."

I allow as how all that sounds good.

"Here's the thing," he says. "You get the girl."

"Beg pardon?"

"The schoolmarm. You get her. Playing a fresh twist off the classic trope, you see."

I make a spittin' motion toward the wastebasket. Kinda thinking things over. Never could abide authors that said things like trope.

So, three shakes of a calf's tail and I'm riding into a half-assed frontier town in (as Evan told me the first day) "Arizona, Montana, some such godforsaken place," dragging a personal history that a hundred or so pages farther along will explain (1) what I'm doing here, (2) why I'm so slow to anger, (3) why I never carry a gun, (4) why I'm partial to sheep, (5) what led to my leaving Abilene, El Paso, Fort Worth or St. Louis, (6) and so on.

Glancing back, I see what looks suspiciously like a guitar wrapped in a flour sack slung across my horse's rump. The horse's name is Challenger, but I vow right then and there that, however long this thing lasts, he'll be George to me. And, yep, we hit a rut in the road and the sack bounces up and comes down with a hollow, thrumming sound. It's a guitar all right.

This could be bad.

Eyes watch from windows as I pass. An old man sitting out front of the general store lifts his hat momentarily to look, then lets it fall back over his face. Someone shoulders a heavy sack into a wagon, sending up dense plumes of white dust. Two kids with whittled wood guns chase each other up and down the street. I can see the knife marks from here. One of the kids has a limp, so he'll be the schoolmarm's, naturally.

Think about it. I've got a guitar on the back of this horse and I'm heading for . . . pulling up in front of . . . yeah, it's the saloon all right.

At least I'm not the sidekick again.

Inside, a piano player and a banjo man are grinding out something that could be "Arkansas Traveller" or "Turkey in the Straw" but probably isn't intended to be either. Seeing my guitar, the banjo man narrows his eyes. He also misses the beat, and his pick skitters out onto the floor, glistening, dark and hard, like a roach.

"Name it," the barkeep says, and for a moment I think this is some kind of self-referential game old Evan's playing, but then I realize the barkeep's just asking what I want. What I want is a nice café au lait, but I settle for "Whiskey" which tastes of equal parts wasp venom and pump-handle drippings. Not to mention that you could safely watch eclipses through the glass it was served in.

The town doc's in there, naturally. He comes up, trying hard to focus, so that his head bobs up and down and side to side like a bird's, to ask if I've brought his medical supplies. Have to wonder what he was expecting. Out here, a knife or two, some alcohol and a saw's about all you need.

The banjo man is still eyeing me as one of the girls, who doesn't smell any better than the doc, pushes into me to say she hasn't seen me around before. A moment later, the musicians take a break, and I swear I can hear Evan clearing his throat, pushing back his chair. Then his footsteps heading off to the kitchen.

So at least I ain't gonna have to play this damn guitar for a while.

We hang out waiting for him to come back, smiling at each other and fidgeting. After a while we hear his footsteps again. (Bastard's got café au lait, wouldn't you know? I can smell it.) Just as those stop, an Indian steps up to the bar. He's wearing an Eastern-cut suit and two gleaming Colts.

"Whiskey," he says, throwing down a gold piece that rings as it spins and spins and finally settles.

"Yes, *sir*."

Nodding to the barkeep, he holds up his glass, dips it in a toast, and throws it back. I notice he's got hisself a *clean* glass. That's when his eyes slide over to me.

"Took you long enough getting here," he says.

Damn.

I'm the sidekick again after all.

⁄

Comeback

Scott returned from the dead last night.

We'll have to keep this on the quiet, naturally. Doors locked, shades drawn. The smell alone would give us away.

I'd watched an old episode of *Buffy*, pee'd, turned out the light and fallen into a sleep filled with (go figure) kangaroos and insurance salesmen, only to wake to the realization that I wasn't alone in bed.

"Don't be afraid," Scott said.

Of him? How could I be? I reached—

"Don't turn on the light just yet." I felt his hand on my face. It had been a long time. The hand was cold. "I couldn't die without you," he said, and either laughed or choked on something. Death hadn't improved his sense of humor.

A police helicopter passed over, scant inches above us from the sound, blinking its single bright eye repeatedly across our yard, jumping fence into the neighbor's. Someone on the run. A disturbance.

Once the helicopter was gone, it got so quiet I could hear

the ice machine in the refrigerator working, two rooms away. "Thank you for coming back," I told him.

"Had to. I have a message for the leaders of all the world's religions." Again the laugh, or whatever it was. "*Nah*." Moonlight dropped through a window onto the floor, like something spilled.

"Miss me?"

More than I could ever say.

And yes, what remained was undeniably my sweetheart and the love of my life. The wink didn't quite come off, since his eyelid wasn't there, but the rest, the half-smile, the head tilt, that was pure Scott.

He reached across and turned on the lamp.

"I see you brought my tools." Scott restored antique watches; I couldn't bear to sell or abandon those tiny screwdrivers, files, anvils, nips and mallets. "Looked about a bit before I came in here. Doesn't seem you brought much else."

I put my hand under the sheets, the whisper of them loud in the quiet room.

"Can you . . . ?"

"No. Sorry."

"It's okay." I leaned my head on his shoulder and breathed deeply. He breathed, I noticed, only before speaking.

"It was a puzzle, finding you."

"But you did."

"I wasn't ever one for quitting. "

"Even now."

"Even now, yes." The laugh again, as his hand gently touched my face. "I remember that stain on the ceiling. Many's the night we lay watching, waiting for car lights."

"So we could make shapes of it."

"Oceans. Protozoans."

"Petroglyphs."

"Tonight it just looks like a stain."

"Maybe."

He turned towards me in bed. "We swore we'd never come back to this dump—remember?"

"They were good days, Scott."

"Early on, yes."

"We were young."

"Poor as fleas on church mice."

I let that ring down. "Coming back here was the only thing that helped. The memories."

"Memories are what you take with you. Isn't that the point?"

"Who the hell knows what the point is? Do you?"

He shook his head.

The police helicopter passed over again, no stabbing light this time.

"Do you have regrets, Maggie?"

"None," I said, "no." I reached and turned off the lamp. All I could see now was beautiful darkness.

◻

Beautiful Quiet of the Roaring Freeway

He always wondered what their stories were.

Maybe they wondered about his too.

He'd look in the rear view, pick up on posturing, body language. Some were just thrill seekers, of course, not much to be said there. Could be this was a onetime thing for them, they'd go home after, slip back into their lives and stay. Others were desperate to find bad and kept looking, whatever the cost. Or they were just bored. Curious what stepping outside things might feel like. Occasionally he'd get a rider who seemed to be protesting some hard-felt lack of freedom, though it was difficult to imagine how they thought that would work, with everything about the rides kept well on the down low. And once in a while he'd get romantics who spent so much time thinking about the old days that they believed they remembered them. Take one's sweet lady or kind gentleman out for a moonlight ride.

These two, he didn't have a clue. His handler had checked them out, naturally. Nothing had wobbled or gone off focus.

The woman was anywhere between ten and twenty years younger, wearing a pearl-gray blouse and a dark business suit expertly cut for comfort over stylishness, hair mid-length, layered. Her companion seemed to have a mild speech defect of some sort. Levin took note of it at the pickup site, and again in the vehicle when repeatedly she leaned close as the man spoke. He was in casual clothes of the kind that likely, being from a tailor's hand, bore no labels. Shirt, sport coat and trousers all were of different colors.

Hardly unexpected, that they'd be what Levin's old man always called people of substance. Midnight rides don't come cheap. Though once Levin had as passenger a dying woman whose family had pooled resources to provide what she'd spoken of with longing all her life, from stories told her by the grandfather who raised her.

The two of them back there now had privacy, of course. The plex was down. No sound carried. Their windows were clear, Levin's to every appearance opaque. From the menu, they had pre-ordered traditional fado, which fed at low volume to front as well as back. Fascinating to watch in the rear view how the music's rhythms crossed and recrossed the couple's own as they turned to look out, shifted in their seats, spoke, waited, listened.

Quarter SW2 was chosen for its population density, guaranteeing high traffic, and for ready access to the freeway. The quarter also hosted a major virtual university, so information of every sort and kind was bouncing and bubbling off the net around here. Another kind of crowd to get lost in.

Carefully matching the speed and flow of other cars on their way upstream, Levin pulled into the go lane. This was the chanciest part. Where they were most likely to get tagged. Levin's actions were smooth, seamless.

Not many could do this.

Soon they were up the ramp and on the big road, eight lanes, moving at a fast clip with all the others, guided by the sure hand and many-leveled mind of Trafcom. Supposed to be, anyway.

Tales of people getting into their cars and taking randomly to the road for great adventures were once a big thing, Levin knew. Right up there with mythologies that seem imprinted in us. Jealous gods, voyages to the rim of the world, unstoppable warriors. One didn't hear about adventures much anymore. What they were doing now, those two in the back, that was about as close as anyone came.

In the next three lanes, vehicles began to slow, first in the closest, then the next, as a single vehicle angled across and through them. Same, then, with adjacent lanes, till the vehicle drew out of sight down one of the red ramps. Trafcom detecting a malfunction, most likely.

Guitar chords sounded as the singer paused, and hung in the air as though trying to hold on, not let go, dwell here. Always interesting, what music got chosen. Did passengers simply check off one of the standard programs? Order something specific? Loud, quiet, lush, mood-drenched? These had picked fado, Portugal's mournful music of fatefulness, loss and lifetime longing.

Levin kept casual watch in the mirror. Whatever the relationship, whatever their story, things were not going well in the back seat. The woman had been looking on as, often instinctively, he made the myriad adjustments and accommodations necessary to echo and fit the patterns set by Trafcom. Now she leaned forward to tap at the plex. Levin motioned towards the combox mounted near her shoulder. She touched the pad.

"You're very good, aren't you?"

We'd all better hope so, he thought. Aloud he said, "Speaking with the driver is not allowed. This was covered at time of purchase."

"Yes, of course. It's just that I have to wonder why someone does what you do. How he might have come to that."

When Levin responded no further, she sat back.

He thought about that old woman again, Lina, whose family pooled their funds for the ride. That one time he *had* spoken, and listened. She'd been a dancer, she told him, a ballerina. Worked all her life to be so perfect in movement, so uniform, as to become almost machinelike. In a sense to remove the human from what she did, and at the same time to fully represent humanity in a way nothing else could. People see us dance, she said, and they think freedom. It isn't freedom, young man, it's absolute engagement.

One of the sensors tripped but instantly disengaged. A routine sweep, then. For the moment they were clear. Somehow the woman picked up on this. She interrupted her companion to speak. He glanced forward, resumed talking. Again Levin had to wonder why the two of them were here, what would bring them to pay a small fortune for the ride, take so great a risk. They gave no evidence of excitement or anticipation. From the look of them this might be an everyday outing, off to work or to do some shopping.

Vehicles began to move in waves and pulses to the right, ever at steady speed, signaling that something was ahead, poor road conditions, an emergency perhaps, with Trafcom redirecting to maintain flow. Just as effortlessly, Levin swung into the wave crossing from his lane. The communal speed dropped—imperceptibly, were it not for instruments, just over one kph. Within minutes the lanes were repopulated. All was back to normal.

Movement took his eye to the mirror as the woman reached for the combox.

"This is it?" she said. And after a moment: "I expected more."

Don't we all, Levin thought.

Then, as though he had been waiting for this single moment, Levin was accelerating. The woman, then the man, looked up. The fado ended on a broken, long-sustained chord. With a two-second pause, no more than a hiccup, traffic parted before them, moved away right and left. Every sensor on the dash red-lined as Trafcom, with a power and a pull almost physical, battered at the vehicle's controls, searching for identification, foothold, purchase.

Levin ignored all signals and alarms. He continued to accelerate. Maybe Trafcom would break through the vehicle's defenses, take control, maybe not. Behind him, the woman slid to the front of her seat. In the bright light of surveillance vehicles closing upon them, her face became beautiful.

New Teeth

He'd been in a hundred like it, maybe a thousand. Pitch-dark streets outside, garbage in doorways, rotting boards on shop windows, a skeletal stray dog or two. Inside was some better. He took one of the half a dozen wobbly stools at the bar, pointed to the beer tap. Man behind nodded and had it there in moments. The liquid sloshed like backwater, settled.

"Live close by, do you?" The speaker wore a thumb-size listening device that could as easily be hearing support, music source, computer or phone link. That was in his left ear, same side as his good arm. The other arm ended just below the elbow. Held the mug in the good hand, worked the handle with the elbow. He was the kind of thin that brought *spindly* to mind. Who knows what that hair might bring to mind. Moss, maybe.

Walsh smiled and sipped his beer.

"Most come down here, they'll be reg'lars." The man feigned attending to something behind the bar, after a bit said, "Be over there, you find need."

Walsh checked the place out in the mirror behind the bar, then swung round on his stool to compare. The duskiness and blur of the old mirror had helped. Took edges away, smoothed the room over, gave it some mystery it didn't have and never would.

He reached back and got his beer, had a healthy swig this time. Slight oily taste to it. Stayed on in the back of your throat, on your tongue.

It's not the guy sitting at the end of the bar with his head down, of course. Or the woman propped against the playbox, light flushing up onto her face. Not the guy stutter-stepping back from the dumper and shakily regaining his chair at the table with two others.

It's the one grinning away and doing verbal back slaps at the gaming table. Of course. What they want most of all is to blend in.

Walsh puts the beer down, stands. It sees him coming and does what they all do, most of them anyway, it just stands there. Knowing that he knows, knowing what he is, why he's here. Six more steps, three quick moves, and it's over.

Walsh goes back to the bar and finishes his beer. No one is speaking, just looking down at the floor.

As he goes out, the woman sitting alone at a table by the door says, very quietly, "Thank you."

∕

Some know, some don't. Some know and pretend not to. The old man, Statler, knew more about them than anyone else, truckloads more, but he didn't know what they are exactly, or where they come from. Some other here, some other now? he always said.

"And it doesn't really matter, does it," he tells Walsh. The kid's twelve, thirteen, wandered in off the streets after living on them for years, stayed a night, stayed another, then just stayed. He'd heard the stories out there on the street, figured they were only boogeymen and Bigfoot dressed up in new garb. "They're here now, more of them every day."

"What do they want?" the kid asks.

The old man peers at him one-eyed through the barrel of a rifle he's broken down for cleaning. "That part's simple. What we all want: to go on existing. However they can."

Hermits, the old man called them. "Like crabs, moving into the abandoned shells of others. 'Cept the shells ain't abandoned at first. That takes a while."

And Walsh wondered for the first time, back then, what it was like to have someone, some *thing*, there with you inside your skull, inside your skin. Did you know from the first, or did the knowledge come slowly? Did you feel the thing growing there, taking over? Did you feel yourself slowly, by pieces, giving way? Going away.

By the time a jumper got the old man, Walsh had already put down dozens of them. Came by one night with a bottle and beer since it'd been a few weeks, saw it in his eyes. It had moved in strong, had a good hold. Using his gestures, the way he talked, but Walsh knew. It did too. Stood there like they do, waiting. No one said thank you that time.

For weeks Walsh has had a floater in his right eye, seeing shapes in the corner of rooms, in half darkness, that weren't there. As he turned into his building he thought he saw a man, a figure, at the top of the stairs, but when he looked straight on, there was no one.

Halfway up them he heard ghanduuj. The door was ajar. His

visitor stood by the V-box running a stubby index finger down the menu.

"Guardian Dorn," Walsh said, "so good to see you again."

Ghanduuj is built on cycles of twenty beats subdivided to every possible permutation. Eight de-escalating sub-climaxes. One of them hit now. The visitor shook his head. "This is what you listen to? Explains a lot."

"Don't suppose you brought dinner?"

Dorn shook his head again, but differently. There seemed to be an entire vocabulary of head shakes accessible to him.

"A courtesy call, one might say. At the suggestion of Magistrate Helm?"

"So the magistrate doesn't wish to see me herself. Good news."

"Of a sort." Dorn thumbed the music off. "When that time comes, I suppose she'll be sending around someone less charming."

"No doubt." Walsh went to the shelves by the sink, fetched down a bottle and glasses, poured. "Will you drink with me, Billy Dorn? For the good old times?"

The visitor took his. "And for the dream of good new times."

They settled in, watched light bleed from the sky as the window went dark, easy with the silence and without need to cover it over, friends by no stretch of language, yet fragilely bound by a thing neither understood.

Walsh snapped on a lamp. "You're hungry? I have udon. Peanuts. Shallots."

He went back to the counter by the sink to start the meal and Dorn followed. "She *will* send someone, you know," Dorn said. "It's only a matter of time."

"Time I can use to get on with my work."

"Killing people."

"What I kill is no longer a person."

"So you believe. Nonetheless it's murder."

"Legally. When the Magistrate sends someone here, for me—that will be different?"

Spiced oil sizzled and jumped in the pan, its smell taking over the apartment, duple and triple rhythms mixed, as in ghanduuj. Walsh threw noodles into the hot skillet, scooped a handful of peanuts and a scallion onto the counter for chopping. Like the body of a guitar, the hollows of the cabinet below amplified the clean strike of knife on countertop. Each stroke was a small door slamming.

"There is no evidence that they exist. You know that," Dorn said later, as they ate.

⟋

Walsh's runners stayed busy that season. They ate well, their clothes got mended and replaced.

He used street kids as spotters. Many of them, the ones who had survived out there, they could feel the difference when no one else could. They'd watch the way a woman walked down the street, take in how a man reached out to open a door or failed to hesitate before stepping off a curb, and nod: That one. And word would come along the line to Walsh.

He put down a whole family of them, five in all—first time that had happened—over the bridge in Greenway, later that week a single mother in Cable Park. He left the one child that hadn't been jumped, put the other one down with the parent. Then a man and wife nine blocks from where he lived. One of them was a full jump, the other fresh and had no idea what was going on.

They all just stood there and waited.

Then one night as he's coming back home Walsh decides he's being followed and diverts. Only one person, he thinks. One of his runners maybe, but no, they'd come right up. He takes the tunnel under Orchid Street, stepping cautiously among the squatters, some of them with cardboard boxes for shelter, ancient shopping bags or backpacks hugged close. His breath plumes out ahead of him. So does that of the man who follows. Not from the magistrate—that one he'd never see. As far as he knows, there is no sense of community or concerted action among jumpers; they inhabit whatever social forms their host claimed. But you can never be sure. Things change. He could be known to them.

He loses the follower finally in the knot of crooked streets around the central train terminal.

Week or two later, it was an old man there before him. Late sixties, seventies, thin puffs of hair at the side of his head, a lot more sprouting from his ears. You didn't see old people much anymore, of course, and Walsh had never before seen one jumped. Did jumpers select? *Could* they? Something he hadn't thought of. Maybe they just dropped into whatever container was available.

He'd been sitting at the table when Walsh slipped the lock, stood when he came in. A single room, table in the far corner, bed in another, two hard plastic chairs, makeshift shelves. Change of clothing hung on nails driven into the wall. A dog as used-up as the man lay sleeping on the bed.

The whole place smelled somehow of meat. The old man? The dog? Half a century of bad and half-rotten food? A flower that looked as though it had struggled from day one to stay alive but was still holding on stood upright in a Coke bottle.

"I've been expecting you," the man said.

Walsh shook his head. "No. You haven't."

"Death is always expected. And to one my age, a comfort. The last good friend you will meet." And he smiled.

Stone crazy, then. The jumper had come across only to find itself in a tangle of cross-wired, blown, burned out circuits.

The old man didn't just stand there, he took a step towards Walsh. Another thing Walsh hadn't seen before. And for a moment, wondering how it was that the man himself, what remained of him, was able to speak—or was it the jumper after all—Walsh hesitated.

The dog looked up, watched, and put its head back down on its paws.

◢

"Are you okay?" Dana's voice.

He hit Accept on the V-box and she came onscreen, eyes narrowing at his image.

"You're just getting up." She was at the office. Dressed for it. Familiar sounds behind her. Morning? Afternoon?

"I could just be going to bed."

"Which would be precious little improvement. We haven't heard from you in ages."

"Or ever."

"People do ask."

"Only to be polite, Blue Girl."

They had worked side by side for almost a year. She was half his age. For months she'd worn nothing but blue. Blue skirts or pants, blue jackets, blue shoes. He always wondered if his use of the nickname was what changed that.

"Same old?" he said.

"What would change?"

"Truth."

Essentially they were a clean-up crew, vetting paperwork done by others before passing it on for documentation and filing. Important paperwork dealing with health care legislation, but still. Days, he worked there. Nights he searched out jumpers. When the jumpers got plentiful, and after he put together his band of spotters, he quit.

It wasn't paperwork, of course, not a scrap of paper anywhere to be seen, just screens and gigabytes, but the name stayed on. So much of life was soft-spoken metaphor, something standing in for something else.

"I do worry over it," Dana said. "There at the end . . . Well, never mind that. But call me from time to time, let me know you're okay. Okay?"

"Will do."

"Won't. But at least think about it?"

How the room could seem smaller afterwards he didn't understand, but it did.

Sometimes at night, when he's not out hunting, when he can't sleep, he listens to arguments coming through the wall from the next apartment. There's a young girl over there, one tacking hard into youthful rebelliousness and scorn for parents, for authority, for the larger society, for all received wisdom and assumptions. The clashes can go for hours. Low-pitched, reined-in voices, feral shouts, slamming doors, silence.

It's not about what you want.

I'm not you.

My house, my rules.

You have to let me make up *my* mind about who I am.

Walsh fell asleep still listening, thinking that four thousand years ago in Athens, a Greek family was probably having the same set-to, using much the same words.

"At what cost?" the old man asks that night in his dreams. Not Statler—the other old man. The one with the dog. He is moving towards Walsh as he speaks. "This thing that you feel you have to do. At what cost?"

"Cost? To whom?" Walsh says.

"Yourself." The man stops. Walsh realizes now that he is blind. His eyes pass over Walsh and fix on a spot to his side. "All of us."

Walsh woke with a sense of—what? Failure? Loss? He lay remembering a woman from his days on the streets, a graffiti artist who worked the edge of the business district, as though she could never cross the line into that half-mile square but was committed to gracing its perimeter. Gray, snaggly hair to her waist, leathery skin. Bit of a legend, really. He'd come upon her one night as she stood by a wall, spray can in one hand, grease pen in the other. A snarl of dark strokes, a swirl or two. "Something in there that wants out," she said without turning her head.

Walsh got up, climbed the landing to the roof. Down in the street a dozen or so blurry shapes scrambled. Lights lashing antenna-like, two patrol cars converged silently on an intersection. A city he moved through each day and night, and he hardly recognized it. *Things change.* For a moment he thought he saw another man, another shape, across from him on the roof: the floater again. He looked up, where a scant handful of stars struggled to show through clouds.

When the time comes, he will not stand and wait.

$\diagup$

Scientific Methods

No one is allowed to write about the university's collider for fear the neighborhood, led perhaps by owners of the cattle ranch half a mile up the road, or of the apple orchards due south, will rise up in arms. No journalists are to be admitted, queries concerning same will be denied, the whole thing's strictly on the QT. Alone at night, one imagines villagers converging on the castle with pitch-forks and lanterns.

Here is what we know: That another world exists, and that if we can but find the tiniest crack it will open itself to us.

Here is what I know: That I must reconcile

1. what Marta said to me this morning, staring into her waffle as though the words were written there
2. growing suspicion that my work is of no consequence
3. the footprint of a gigantic corporation

There's an equation in there somewhere. Equations being the one true and lasting beauty in this world.

(In the interest of full disclosure I should add, above, that this other world might just as well engulf as enrich us.)

Meanwhile, moments of the day trickle into the blender, hit the stove and sizzle.

"You missed the meeting," A.G. says.

He waits. Water glugs in the cooler. Swallowed air, a void, rises to the top and is gone.

"Glad to hear it."

"The problem of secondary categorization was addressed."

"Addressed, forwarded, and returned to sender, I'm sure—as always."

"B.R. took attendance." Our beloved manager. Third-rate scientist to bureaucrat between one recent Friday and the next.

"Then at least *someone* got something out of it."

"Not much of a company man, are you, T.M.?"

He swings hard right to the aisle as though in the single dance step he knows and ambles away, head abob over cubicle walls, wearing his yellow Friday t-shirt. The front is bare. The back reads

CHAOS
THE FINAL STRUCTURE

Physicists. A fun-loving lot.

Here's what we do: We take a particle that is so small it's mostly imagination. We whirl it around till it's going faster than is possible and we push it into another particle to see what happens. We do this Tuesdays and Thursdays at 2:14 AM. We have all manner of ideas what will happen. Some of these ideas turn out to be true.

Here's what I do: I pull out my handheld and type in *I will try to be a better person.* Thumbs hover as I think. Who? I send it to myself.

It's casual Friday, B.R.'s premiere contribution to productivity and worker morale, so the halls teem with cargo shorts, fake jerseys and flip-flops, B.R.'s second contribution being the monstrous TV in the break room where Dana (substitute halter top and sweats for above) spends most of her time. She'll sit in there forever, suddenly jump out to her cubicle and click keys at light speed for five or ten minutes, then go back. As far as I can tell, she never watches the TV or for that matter even knows what's on. When I asked her, she told me it was like being immersed in water, like floating. And that it cut out all the other noise. Let her think clearly.

Today she wears a single earring that's heavy with brass and hangs to her shoulder. Her head tips ever so slightly to that side.

Thinking clearly. I sort of remember that. Too much stuff in my head now. Like boxes full of old clothes and photos and untouched birthday gifts stacked half to the ceiling in the spare room. You just *know* you'll use it all someday.

I look up as R.K. emerges from the supply room with an ink cartridge clutched between thumb and first finger. He never shuts doors. Supply room, phone room, break room, it doesn't matter, he steps away leaving half an inch of daylight between door and frame. The rest of us have got so used to following along, closing doors, that we don't much notice we're doing it anymore.

I do have to wonder what use he might have for an ink cartridge, as we dwell exclusively in cyberland and never print anything out, endlessly skyhopping data from desktop to remote to handheld or smartphone.

Fridays, the local bagpipe brigade in an amazement of plaid crosses the plaza below us on its ceremonial way to Main

Street and City Park. Ceremonial of what, no one quite re-members, but after lunch everyone's standing at the window up front watching, albeit that, from three stories up, through double-paned glass, all we can hear is what sounds like a huge mosquito. And drums, of course.

Ah, the spinning of mallets. The rise and fall of knobby knees. The swing and sway of mighty sporrans.

They've been doing this, I'm told, for eighty-plus years; some of those now marching are great-grandsons of original members. Tribalism is not dead. Nor tradition.

Nor am I, though this year's scan, from last Tuesday, does not look good. "Definitely something there," Doctor Freeman tells me. He points to what looks like a spill of milk on the black film with its many ghosts, moves one finger in a close circle. The tumor of which I was delivered nine years ago may no longer be an only child.

More tests, then. And I've always been good at taking tests. Back as an undergrad I rarely read assignments on subjects in which I had no interest, English, sociology and so on, and rarely studied, but did well on mid-terms and finals.

Mid-term or final, I'll ace this one too.

J.T. walks by behind me in the corridor between cubicles, speaking to no one that I can see. Yes, he says. And again, fur-ther along, quieter now: Yes. I sit here as the second yes speeds down the corridor to where I sit waiting to see what will happen.

Annandale

Everything broke off from the main roads about twelve miles outside town. I bounced over rutted ancient asphalt for better than an hour thinking of the stories and lives I was leaving behind and pulled into Annandale at 7:08 in the morning.

I was going to see a dead friend.

On the way, I drove through miles of dead and decaying animals by the side of the road, armadillos, bobcats, possums and raccoons. It hadn't affected animals at first, when the billybobs came, but it was spreading to them.

The car was a museum piece, a late 20th-century Fiat curated and kept in a secret garage with three others, all of similar vintage and functional, by one of the generals. I'd had eyes on it for some time, lest the need arise.

My father was a hunter. Many's the mid-morning as a child I stood out by the brick barbeque pit watching him gut and skin the squirrels, dove, rabbits and quail he'd brought in earlier from the woods just beyond our house. There wasn't much money in our part of the country, almost none in fact, and none of it ours. The game was much of what we lived on. He'd throw entrails and skin down the hill behind the barbeque pit. Our dogs would climb down to eat them.

No dogs here now, I thought as I drove down Manor Road into the heart of Annandale, such as it was. Little activity on the streets, a jacked-up VW with light dancing off the chrome of its open engine, a pickup with corrugated steel welded to fenders and hood, three or four bicycles fitted with baskets fore and aft. Windows and doors along Main were shuttered with rough-cut plywood slabs, sidewalks heaved up and jaggedly broken like artist's renderings of shifting tectonic plates. The old train station at the nether end of Main, in my childhood become a museum of the region's past in a failed attempt to give the station and town new life, had chains with padlocks on the doors and broken windows through which one could see pigeons fluttering about inside.

Pigeons had left their mark, too, outside Gray's Hardware where for decades men sat smoking and swapping small talk as wives and children shopped along the street. Bench, sidewalk and window casings were gone white with droppings from pigeons gathered by dozens on the broken lattice of the awning above.

Hard to believe I'd lived here once. And now, on the move, just as hard to believe how I'd clung to life in the ruined body of my adopted city after the billybobs came and everyone, everything, around me began dying.

The old diner at the high end of Main was, remarkably enough, open, so I stopped there. It was the shape and size of the railway cars on display down by the train station, booths along one side, lunch counter running the length of the other. Two men sat far apart at the counter with mugs of coffee. A head tilted into sight in the pass-through kitchen window as I entered. Moments later a door close by swung open and when the head, body attached now, asked what it could do for me, I said coffee would be great.

"Let me get a fresh pot started," he said. Then to the others: "You boys be up for refills, am I right?"

As he set about doing so, I took the stool nearest the door.

"Not much passing-through goes on around here," the guy five stools down said.

"Know what you mean." The blackboard by the kitchen window had daily specials chalked on, beef stew, spaghetti w/ balls, fresh greens. Looked like they'd been there a while. "As I was coming in on the old county road I saw the hospital's shut down." They'd always kept bodies there, in a back room on the first floor, nearest thing the town had to a morgue.

"Been that way, what—" He glanced at the man further down for verification. "—five, six years?"

"Least."

He turned back to me. "You're from around here?"

"Long time ago."

"Everything's a long time ago. You looking for medical, closest thing we've got now's old Doc Boggs' office out on—"

"You mean Doc's still alive?"

"Was yesterday. Mostly it's children and old folks get taken there towards the end. The rest . . ."

Why bother was what he meant. They were breathing dead.

We sat drinking our coffee. The radio was on in the kitchen, an oldie station of some kind. It cut out every once in a while, then lurched back on at a higher volume before settling in. Station problems or the radio set itself, hard to say.

"Coming in from where?" the man five stools down asked, and I told him.

"Any better there?"

"Not really."

All three nodded. I told them goodbye and when I tried to pay the owner he said no need, he had all the money and political doubletalk he could use—what could he do with any of it?

Doc's place didn't look much better than the hospital or boarded-up stores downtown. Cue spooky music as vines take over walls second by second and portions of the house give way like shattered bones. Eerily, the lawn was freshly mown, the windows clean and clear. No one answered when I knocked, so I went in. The front room was filled with pallets, at least twelve of them, on which lay aged men and women, some of them breathing heavily, others barely. Babies and infants in much the same condition and on similar improvised beddings occupied the next room. Beyond that was the kitchen, where Doc stood over an ancient gas stove.

"With you in a shake," he said, "just fixing some breakfast for those can eat."

I watched his hands feel along the stove top, pots and utensils and when moments later he turned, it confirmed what I suspected. Both eyes were white with cataracts. He was blind, or nearly so. A blob of oatmeal dropped from the spoon he held.

"Now. Here to help, are you?"

"I'm here to claim a body."

"Help yourself then, many as you might want. They're out back, in the shed."

"Just one, Edgar Foley."

He nodded. "That one's not with them. Him I have upstairs, bedroom at the back. You know he was dug in, doing what he could, right? Brought in a lot of those you walked past, cared for them, before it took him too."

"He was like that."

"He was. Not so much early on in his life, from what he told me, but later, you bet. Close friend of yours?"

"*Friend* doesn't begin to say it."

"Two of you stayed in touch?"

"In a manner of speaking."

Doc stepped up close and stared intently into my face. I had no idea what he could or might see there. "Do I know you, young man?"

"You brought me into this world. Mabel Levine was my mother."

"Sweet past . . . You're Jack."

"Yes, sir."

"Hard behind the resistance, people said back in the day. Planning, executing. The town had pride in you."

"I was underground, then above it but still out of sight. While Ed was helping the fallen. We find our own way in the dark."

"Some do."

"I'm not with the government any longer."

"Not much of one to be with."

"There's that."

Doc had gone back to set the oatmeal pot off the burner. He'd failed to turn off the fire under it. I walked over and did so.

"Ed and I served together, went through a lot. It got so we didn't need to talk, we'd see what needed to get done and go whatever way was best to do it. Like somehow we knew the shape of what the other was thinking, how he felt. That never left, that open space between us, not even afterwards, when we went our separate ways. Just get clear of the world's noise and here's that other life beside yours."

After a moment, Doc nodded. His hands, I saw now—why not before?—were trembling.

"Two weeks back, I felt that again," I said, "after many years. The other life beside mine. Ed's life. I was with him from then on, with him when he died."

"In spirit."

"I suppose."

"I am so very sorry, son."

A sound came from the front room, the beginning of a scream, before it cut off.

"I'll go up and get him now, if that's okay with you."

"Please. And I'd best go see to my patients."

His body ravaged for weeks by the alien virus, there wasn't a lot of Edgar left. But I carried my dead friend back out into the world that would soon belong expressly to the billybobs, sat him beside me in the Fiat, and drove away. It was a beautiful bright day, clouds moving lazily along the horizon.

In spirit, Doc had said. And yes, the spirits of those gone are about us everywhere. They once flew and surged and faltered and now are fallen. We're little more than spirits ourselves, those of us who are left.

"Will you hear my bedtime story for humanity?" I ask my dead friend.

In the beginning, I said, there were two gods. One created the world, the other created mankind. They sat back proud of their work, what they'd done. Then the first said: Yours will never amount to anything.

I guess she was right.

▱

Dayenu
A novella

Dayenu. A song that's part of the Jewish
celebration of Passover:
"It would have been enough for us."

1.

At 10:36 as I'm listening to accounts on the radio of a plane lost over the Arctic Sea, the noise from within the trunk gets to be so annoying that I stop the car, open up, and whack the guy with the cut-down baseball bat I stowed under the front seat. The ride's a lot better after that. They never find the plane.

Where I've pulled off is this little rise from which you can see the highway rolling on for miles in both directions, my very own wee grassy knoll. The trees off the road are at that half-and-half stage, leaves gone brown closer to the ground, those above stubbornly hanging on. Because of Union Day there's little traffic, two semis, a couple of vans and a pickup during the time I'm there, which is the only reason I'm risking everything to be out here and on the road taking care of one last piece of business. Even the government's mostly on hold.

What they never understood, I'm thinking as I get back in the car, what it took me so long to understand, is that after rehab I became a different person. Not as in some idiotic this-changed-my-life blather, or that last two minutes of screen drama with light shining in the guy's eyes and throbs of music. *Everything* changed. How the sky looks in early morning, the taste of foods, longings you can't put a name to. Time itself, the way it comes and goes. Learning all over how to do the most basic things, walk, hold onto a glass, open doors, brush teeth, tie shoes, put your belt on from the right direction—all this reconfigures the world around you. A new person settles in. You introduce yourself to the new guy and start getting acquainted. It can take a while.

An hour later I make the delivery and go about my business, not that there is any. They'd got too close this time and I'd gone deeper to ground, pretty much as deep as one can burrow. The gig was a hold-over from before, timing rendered it possible, so I took the chance. Messages left in various dropboxes now would grow up orphans.

I was staying on the raw inner edge of the city, a gaza strip where old parts of town hang on by their fingernails to the new, in a house with rooms the size of shipping crates. Tattoo-and-piercing parlor nearby, four boarded-up houses like ghosts of mine, an art gallery through whose windows you can see paintings heavy on huge red lips, portions of iridescent automobiles, and imaginary animals.

Nostalgia, dreamland, history in a nutshell.

The house owner supposedly (this gleaned from old correspondence and visa applications) was away "hunting down his ancestry," driven by the belief that once he knows about his great-great grandfather, his own blurry life will drift into focus. So here I am, with every item on the successful lurker's shopping list in place: semi-abandoned neighborhood, evidence of high turnover, no one on the streets, irregular or nonexistent patrols, no deliveries, few signs of curiosity idle or otherwise.

A week or so in, it occurred to me that the neighborhood had this fairy tale thing going. Grumpy old man half a block south, bighead ogre seen peering out windows of the house covered with vines, guy with cornrows who resided at the covered bus stop and could pass for a genie, even a little girl who lived down the lane.

Look at the same frame sideways, of course, and it goes immediately dark: poverty, political pandering, ineptitude, dispossession. Where you watch from, and how you look, dictates what you see.

A cascade of strokes, they told me. Infarctions. Areas of tissue death brought on by interruptions in blood supply and oxygen deprivation—like half a dozen heart attacks moved far north.

No problem, they said. We'll go in and fix this.

So they did.

⁄

They came for me at 4 AM. No traffic or other sounds outside; the curfews were in place. And nothing more than a promise of light in the sky. The third step of the second landing creaked. I made sure of that with a bit of creative carpentry when I moved in.

Four of them. I counted the creaks. Then was out the window and down, gone truly to ground, by the time the last one hit the landing.

We wait to be gathered, my uncle always said. Tribally, commercially, virtually, finally. Uncle Cage disappeared when I was eight, in one of the myriad foreign lands where we indulged what were then called police actions. Hard upon that, his footprints and after-image began to leak away, public records, photographs, rosters. Within a matter of weeks he no longer existed.

Nothing in this old part of town had been planned. The alleyway in which I found myself was no exception; it simply came into being as buildings grew around it. Doorways, jury-rigged gates and dog-legged side paths could lead nowhere. But exits abounded. I took one at random, looking back to where their cars (always two of them, it seemed, always dark gray) sat at curbside, still and featureless as skulls.

We wait to be gathered.

$\triangle$

That day, days before, the wind blew hard, tunneling down through the streets of the city bearing tides of refuse. Drink containers, bits of printout, feather and bone, scraps of clothing. Birds, mostly hawks, stayed put on building tops, electing not to launch themselves into the fray as, overhead, clouds collided and the large ate the small. I was on one of those building tops too, looking down at protestors who had gathered outside People's Hall, protestors largely in their late teens or early twenties, with a sampling from the next generation up sprinkled among them. Just over a hundred, I'd say, though news reports doubled that figure.

The police had military-issue equipment: weapons, body armor, full automatics, electrics. They waded into the kids, stunned a number of them, gassed the rest, now had them facedown on the ground roughly in squares.

There are no right angles in nature.

We're never too far from the ground. My uncle again.

Watching events below so closely, I had failed to notice the drone hovering nearby, took note of it only when one of the hawks launched from a rooftop. The hawk hit hard. Its talons scrabbled for a hold but, finding no purchase, it flew on. Unable to right itself, the drone crashed into the side of a building. Though not before it had scanned me and dialed it in.

◢

Tulips.

In 17th century Holland, Uncle Cage told me, a single bulb of the rare *Semper Augustus* sold for the price of a good house. The tulip craze geared up in November 1636, ran its course, and burned itself out by February of the next year, forever a lesson on inflated markets, fabricated desire and greed of a sort not so much unlearned as endlessly learned and forgotten.

I was seven and had no idea what he was talking about. This was a year or so before he was supposed to come back for a visit, for shore leave. Before he disappeared. Before he got gathered.

I had no idea what he was talking about, but I did have memories of earlier stories, stories that would adhere over time to experiences of my own, form a latticework upon which hung notions of life untempered by slogans, manipulation, and misdirection.

◢

I took breakfast at a Quick'n'Easy, street name Queasy, directly across from the fast rail's inner loop, watching passengers flow onto the platform then drain into the maw of the cars or out onto the streets.

An abandoned building nearby, once a pharmacy, bore an arc of spray-painted letters on its front: REBORN. Another farther along, faded red and yellow colors suggesting it had once been a bodega, read BELIEVE. Christians come into the neighborhood at night and leave their mark, evaporate like dew.

I'd barely settled in at a window seat on the 6:56 Express when the aisle seat beside me filled. We picked up speed; station, sky and buildings outside ran together in a single blurred banner. The light on the camera at the front of the car blinked steadily. I kept my face averted as though looking out the window. Not that this would help all that much, should they engage recognition software.

"Sorry to keep you waiting," I said without turning to my seat mate.

"Two hours, a smidge less. About as I expected. This was your most likely egress."

"You ran a sim?"

"No need. The dogs were closing in, I knew where, I had absolute confidence they'd fail. There was a time we thought alike."

"You might easily have called in the dogs yourself. Primed the pump."

"Ah, but that would lack subtlety. Not to mention it would leave my size ten footprints scattered about digitally. Still, there it was. And when was I likely ever to have another chance to find you?"

Security came through the car randomly checking, a young woman shiny with purpose, uniform pants pressed blade-sharp, and we stopped talking. Outwardly calm, within I was anything but. Flee if possible, fight if not. But she passed us by. Moments later the train slowed almost to a stop as we drew abreast of the war memorial. Passengers went about their business, chatting to companions, working or browsing on links. One woman's eyes never left the wall. She could not see the name, but she knew it was there. Husband? Sibling? Child? As the last row of names crawled by, the train regained speed. At the border between municipalities, guards waved us through.

We went down, temporarily, at West End Station. Sniffers had flagged probable contraband—illicit drugs or explosives, usually—so trains were held and passengers offloaded to the platform. We'd scarcely lined up behind the sensor gates when a young man near the end broke and ran, only to stop moments later as though he'd run into an invisible wall—the first time I'd seen the new electrics in action. Guards unsheathed a wafer-thin stretcher, rolled him bonelessly onto it, and bore him away. Soon we were on the move again.

Warren waited till a teenaged Asian passenger, belt and backpack straps studded with what looked to be ancient revolver casings, passed.

"Here."

I took what he held out, a shape and weight familiar to my hand. Its cover creased and worn though it had to be new.

"A new name, history, vitals, the data manipulated just enough that scans won't flag it, but it's basically you. Most anywhere in the city and surround, these will suffice. You'll want to stay away from admin buildings, information centers." He turned to the window. "This would be your stop."

The announcement came then over the speakers. All our grand technology, and station calls still sound like hamsters gargling.

"Use the papers if you wish. If not, dispose of them. On the chance that you use them, Frances looks forward to seeing you."

I turned back and motioned for him to follow.

We're sitting in a foxhole in some country with too many vowels in its name. Officially this is a TBH, Transport Battle Habitat, and doesn't have much of anything to do with foxholes, but that's what we call it. Made of some mystery plastic that goes hard when you inflate it and soft again when you go the other way. Full stealth optics: bends and reflects light to blend with the surround or disappear into it—woodland, plains, whatever. Desert's harder, of course, but you could almost feel the poor thing struggling, doing its best.

Fran is sniffing at an RP she just tore into. The pack itself looks like jerky or tree bark. A meaningless script of letters and numbers on it but no clue what waits inside. She tries to break off a piece of whatever it is and can't, pulls the knife out of her boot.

"Adventure," I say. "Suspense."

"Hey, chewing on this at least will give me something to do for half an hour." We hear the wheeze and hollow grunt of shells striking not too far off. "The boys are playing again."

"Ding dong the witch ain't dead."

"Just polishing her teeth."

"Shiny!"

Lots of time to talk out there. I know about her favorite toy when she was four or five, a plastic submarine with a compartment you filled with baking soda to make it dive and surface, dive and surface. The head made of a carved coconut with seashells for eyes and ears. Her first kiss—from a boy twice her age whose hand crawled roughly into her shorts. The twin brother who died in a bombing, in the coffeeshop across the street from the college where he taught, when she was in boot camp.

"Everybody was going," she said when she told me about that. "My cat died. My brother. Our old man. Ever feel surrounded?"

I waited for a shell to hit, said "Nah" when one did.

Timing is everything.

She looks out the gun slot of the foxhole. "Dogs'll be next," she says.

The dogs were everywhere back then. Genetically manipulated, physical and mental augmentations. Ten or twelve of them would spill up over the horizon and surge towards you. Nothing short of heavy artillery stopped them. Even then, what was left of them, half dogs, forequarters, kept coming. Most of the time they couldn't see the foxholes but knew they were there—smelled them, sensed them.

These do what we hope: circle us twice, snuffle ground, sniff air, do it all again and move on.

"Damn things give me the willies every time," Fran says.

"They're supposed to. Bring you up against the elemental, the savage, within yourself."

"Deep waters, college boy. Good to see all that schooling wasn't wasted."

"Most of it was. But knowledge is like cobwebs, get close enough, some stick."

Our coms crackle. Go orders. Moments later we're over the top, on our way to finding the elemental and savage within ourselves.

⊿

At night Foragers come out, looking for food, cast-off clothing, machine parts, citizens marooned for whatever reason in their world—anything they can use. Theirs is a mission of salvage, scooping up leftovers, cast-offs, the discarded. They decline the housing, employment, health care and securities guaranteed to all, choosing to live invisibly, perilously, and when every few years the government extends offers of amnesty, those offers go ignored.

Walking away from the station into thinner ground and air, we passed a number of Foragers who looked on, even followed a bit, before concluding it unwise to approach.

Warren watched as one, a woman in her late teens or early twenties, face pale above an ankle-length dark overcoat, military issue, took a final look and withdrew. "Interesting lives," he said.

"They're a part of you, deep inside, that longs to scream *No.*"

"Perhaps not so deep as you imagine." He touched a wall, ran his hand along it. Dark grit fell from the hand when he took it away. "How did we come to live in a world where everything is something else?"

"Other than what it seems? We've always lived there."

"Then how do choices get made?"

"Faith."

"Now there's something you can hold onto." He pulled out a link, looked for a moment at the screen, and replaced it. "Our plan to protect Frances—"

"By staging her death."

"—was solid, with high probability of success."

"Not that it would ever occur to others that it was a ploy."

He met my eyes, an action intended to register sincerity and directness but in effect defensive.

"*High probability* means you ran sims," I said, "as many times as it took for someone to get onto those runs."

"Of course."

"Then you had the tag. Trawled out and put them down. It wasn't about protecting Fran."

We walked on. Pavement out here was everywhere cracked, fractured into multiple planes, grass and weeds growing from the fissures like trees on a hundred tiny hills.

"Afterwards," Warren said, "she simply chose *not to*—much as you did."

Thinking I heard footsteps, I put out an arm to halt us. We stood quietly, breathing slowly. Nothing more came. "Do you know where she is?"

"No. Nor, we trust, do those attempting to kill her."

"You've intel?"

He shook his head. "Five words to a secure address. *Introduce me to your friend?*"

"A safe word."

"And her way of asking for you. A request she would make only . . ."

Around us, like his sentence, the city trailed off, neither quite there nor absent. Heaps of refuse that looked to be undisturbed. Few sign of rats or other rodents—larger beasts who'd rarely venture closer to the city saw to that.

◢

College days. Stray bunches of us had got our heads filled with notions of retrieving history, scrubbing away the years, getting back to common ground we'd misplaced. Music became a part of this; for about five minutes I played at being a musician. Fell in quickly with Sid Coleman, and while I wasn't ever much good and wasn't going to be, I could bite into a rhythm and never let go. We started out playing for parties, college gigs and such. Later, it was mostly protest meetings.

Sid steamed with frustration from the get-go. What he wanted to do was talk politics but what everyone else wanted was for him to bring his guitar and sing. He had started out with old-time mountain music, discovered calypso and Memphis jug bands, slid into home base with songs against what we started calling the forever wars. He sang right up to the day he got his notice. That day he put his guitar away for good.

Sid and his crew were chowing down on a breakfast of beer and RPs when mortar shells struck. Eight were killed. And while Sid escaped further injury, the blasts took his hearing. This was a couple of borders over from where we are now. It's all the same war, he used to sing, they just move it from place to place.

—Hang on, Fran said, I need to pee. She checked with the infrared scope for all clear and stepped out. Got back and said Okay . . .

That's it. There isn't any more.

Oh.

But there was.

Years later, back home, I ran into Sid on the street. I could see in his face that he didn't remember me, though he claimed to. He wore fake fatigues, the kind they sell at discount stores, and bedroom slippers. His hair was carefully combed, with a sheen of oil that smelled rank. Don't get out much, he said.

One social engagement on my calendar every month. On the 15th, 0900 to the minute, the government check lands in my account. No fanfare, no fail, there it is, egg plopped in the nest. And there I am too, waiting to claim my money.

Someone hands you a gun, you don't check it out before you use it, be sure of its function, you're a fool. Same with false papers. Next morning I crossed the southeast border into Palms, a city with no industry or trade centers and of scant strategic interest, populated as it is by the aged afloat on their pensions.

Cities, like the civilizations they reflect, find their rhythm. Their surges, falls. Areas within falter, decline and bottom out, open to new strains of inhabitants and push their way back up. Palms for now was on hold, a single sustained note.

From town's center I walked out to the grand artificial lake where picnic tables, benches, and teeter-totters squatted at eight-meter intervals around clear water. Teeter-totters, one assumes, for visiting grandchildren, though that day there were none. Plenty of elderly folk at the tables or sitting with feet in the water on low-slung walls, people a generation or two younger standing by. Caretakers.

I ended up back in town at a sparsely populated outdoor café, server and barista of an age with those around. Bob, the server, put me in mind of old-time French waiters, professional mien and mantle donned with his apron. The barista's demeanor came from warmer climes; she tapped on cup bottoms, swiveled about, triggered the steamer in syncopated bursts as she worked. Mildred's a peach, Bob said, directing his gaze briefly that way when I commented.

A couple I'd estimate to be in their eighties sat across from one another at a table nearby, each with a link propped before. She'd key in something on hers, he'd look at his. They'd both look up and smile. Then it was his turn.

Children? Images from long ago—a vacation on the big

island before the embargos, places they'd lived, concerts and celebrations attended, their younger selves?

Even stolid Bob registered their happiness, careful not to interrupt but repeatedly locating himself close by lest they need something.

A frail-seeming man in eyeglasses sat reading an actual book whose title I eventually made out to be *A History of Radical Thought*. Interesting, that use of the indefinite article, I thought, *a* instead of *the*; one had to wonder at the content. There could be so many such histories.

When Bob set down a tea cake at another table, the woman there waited for him to walk away then quickly dipped her head and with one hand in half a moment sketched a shape in the air before her: silent prayer, and what few would recognize as the sign of the cross.

Across the street, in a park bordered on the far side by off-set stands of trees, two women in sundresses, a style I recalled from childhood, were flying a kite made to look like a huge frog and awash with bright yellows, crimson, metallic blues. The runner had just let go the kite; both laughed as the frog took to sky.

Smelling of fresh earth, rich and dark, the coffee was good. I had three cups, took another walk round the lake, and re-mounted the train without challenge or incident. On the trip back, mechanical or guidance problems delayed us, and it grew dark as we reached the city, lights coming on about us, curfew close enough to give concern. Officials waited on the platform to issue safe passes. Elsewhere, automatic weapons cradled in their arms, soldiers who looked to be barely out of adolescence patrolled.

2.

So, there I am in a room, rooting about in the few personal belongings left behind, listening for footsteps outside in the hall or coming up stairs. How did I arrive here? We wonder that all our lives, don't we?

It was as much the idea of a room as it was a room. Plato and Socrates might have stood at the door arguing for days. A single small window set high, its plastic treated so that light blossomed as it passed through, flooded the room with virtual sunshine. From one wall a lower panel let down to become a bed, another panel above to serve as table or desk.

Where a man lives and what's inside his head, they're mirrors of one another, my trainers said. In which case there shouldn't be a whole lot going on in Merrit Li's. And if I had the right person, I knew *that* wasn't true.

My inventory disclosed a packet of expired papers and passes bound together in a drawer, a thin wallet containing recent travel visas, a drawerful of clothes, some disposable, some not, all of them dark and characterless. On his link I found itineraries and receipts, forty-six emails that seemed to be business related, though what business would be impossible to discern, and a young adult novel about the Nation Wars.

Elsewhere about the room, apportioned to the innards of various appliances, a Squeeze, a cooker, a coffee maker, I found what could only be the components of a stunner, cast in a hard plastic I'd not seen before, doubtless unkennable to scanners.

Immediately I became aware of a presence in the doorway behind me. There'd been no warning sounds, no footsteps. Right. So he had to be who and what I thought.

"We have mutual friends," I said, turning.

"Else you wouldn't be here."

Older than myself by a decade and more, conceivably old enough to remember the wars he'd been reading about. No sign of recognition at the safe word. Stance and carriage, legs apart, shoulders and hips in a line, confirmed other suspicions. Military.

I glanced up from his feet at the same time he did so from mine. Anticipating attack, one sees it begin there.

"Your belongings remain as they were," I said.

He nodded. Waited.

"Three days ago you were in Lower Cam, at a train stop where an attack took place. Two citizens were injured. The target, Frances di Palma, fled."

"Leaving a body behind her. That one not a bystander."

He held out both hands to signal non-aggression and, at my nod, stepped to the console to dial open the built-in screen. Habit—and of little benefit should we be on lens, but one takes the path available.

A spirited discussion of the city's economic status bloomed onscreen: female moderator, one man in a dark suit, one in a sky blue sweater. It's really quite simple, assuming you have

the facts, the suit-wearer said. The other's expression suggest
ed that not once in his life had he encountered anything other
than complexity, nor could he anticipate ever doing so.

"You believe I was there to take her down," Merrit Li said.

"Yes."

"I was there, but to a different purpose than you suppose.
She is in fact a mutual friend. I know her as Molly."

◢

Rueful Tuesday, two days before. I had the windows dialed down
while watching a feed on vanishing species. I sat back, dialed the
window up, the screen down, to look across at the next building.
Uncle Carl used to tell me a story about how this early jazz man,
Buddy Bolden, threw a baby out the window in New Orleans
and a neighbor leaned out his window and caught it. That's about
how close we were.

For a moment I could make out moving shapes over there,
people, before they dialed down *their* window.

I had punched back in for the sad tale of vanished sea ot-
ters and was remembering how when we'd first come here to
the city, half-jokingly calling ourselves settlers, jumpy with
wonder, with the effort and worry of fitting in, there'd been a
linkstop showing disaster movies round the clock. World after world ravaged by giant insects, tiny insects, momentous
storms, awakened deep-sea creatures, carnivorous plants, science, our own stupidity.

With no forewarning, otter, shore and sea contracted, si-
phoned down to a crawler.

Warren's face above.

"This," he said, then was gone.

Rosland, time stamp less than an hour ago. A train stop. Single tracks up- and downtown, a dozen people waiting. Strollers, shufflers. Solitary busker playing accordion, license pasted to his top hat, little movement otherwise. Then suddenly there was.

A man walked briskly towards a woman waiting by the uptown track. She turned, transformed at a breath from citizen to warrior, everything about her changing in that instant. She shifted legs and feet, leaned hard left as he fired, followed that lean into full motion.

Moments later, the man lay on the platform, face turned to the camera.

Then another face glancing back, gone as its owner sprinted up the walkway Fran had vanished into.

Merrit Li's face.

Whereupon Warren's returned.

"We think there were two other incidents, but this is the first we've had surveillance."

"Fran took one of the attackers down."

"Cleanly."

"The second attacker followed her."

"In the tunnel they're off lens. We lost them. Nothing topside, nothing on connected platforms."

"Any luck flagging her follower?"

"Check your drops. The bundle I sent should help with that."

⏐

"We fought together at Kingston," Merrit Li said. "Deep penetration. She had the squad."

Doing what Rangers do.

"Not many walked away, either side." He thumbed the sound on the room's screen up a notch. "With the years, details have taken on a life of their own. You know the song?"

Two of them, actually. The official version, Kingston as a triumph of patriotism and the human spirit; the other underscoring the battle's death toll, social cost, and ultimate pointlessness.

"Three of us came out of the fire. Two walking, one on Molly's shoulder."

Onscreen discussion of city economy had given way to the latest stats on immigration. Full-color graphs rolled across the screen. Authorities revoiced the stats and graphs: a marked uptick in Citizen Provisionals from rural regions far south, this fueled by border disputes among neighboring city-states. Graphics and voice-over were out of synch. Technician error, I thought. Then for a moment before getting shut down, voice and content changed drastically. Revisionist overdubs. Official news reestablished itself.

Li pointed to the screen, one of the southern borders. Drones from a couple generations back floated above scattered groups of ragged troops and rioters.

"I'm supposed to be there. Just about now, my CO is discovering I'm not."

Even those you never see cast shadows. What I'd had were forests of filters and firewalls, limited access to public records, and no idea at all to whom his allegiance belonged, or if he might be off the grid entirely. But I also had Li's face, by extrapolation his body volumes, and the way his body moved. It had taken me the best part of the two days since Warren dialed in with the clips, and a sum of chancy data diving, to find him.

"I assume your story varies little from my own," Li said.

"Little enough."

He waited a moment, then went on.

"One of my links stays on free scan, reach-and-grab for anything that hints of undisclosed military activity. Tagged one that felt half solid. Then another came through ringing like bells. Not much to doubt there. A takedown, and good—but it didn't work. And seeing how it unrolled, I knew why. Molly. That first time too, I figured, so now they'd come at her twice and she put them down. They'd be getting ready to kick it into overdrive."

"You have any idea why she was targeted?"

"It's not like we were sending Union Day cards to one another, with a nice write-up about our year."

"Right. Time to time, I'd hear things. She married and had a family up in Minnesota or Vancouver. She was consulting for or riding herd on private companies. She'd taken up teaching. Until last week, as far as I knew, she was dead."

"While on assignment."

"What we all heard. Turns out we weren't the only ones."

Li didn't react, didn't ask where that came from. The pieces were falling together in his mind. "A crawler," he said.

"Followed by full-frontal assault. Once that closed down, Fran elected to stay off chart."

"The moves on her could be flashback from that."

"Could be."

"And we don't know who the crawler found."

"What we know between us doesn't take up much space in the world."

Li glanced back at the screen. Forsaken drones. Ragtag troops and rioters. "Everything's like paper folded so many times you can't tell what it is anymore."

I remembered Warren's rhetorical *How did we come to live in a world where everything is something else?*

"Molly called out to you," Li said.

"Relayed a message with a trigger word." I told him much of the rest as well.

"Wanted you at her back."

"As you said, they'll be stepping it up."

"And you came to me."

Yes.

"So now she has us both."

"Or will have."

Li pulled his duffel from a shelf by the door. "Not much here I can't leave behind. Give me ten minutes. Molly, you, me. Damn near have the makings of a volunteer army here, don't we? A militia—just like that hoary old piece of 1787 paper said."

3.

What I remember is questions, questions that should have been easy enough but weren't, and I had no idea why. What is today's date? Do you know where you are? It took time before I realized the voices were speaking to me. They were voices beamed in from some far-off world that had nothing to do with me, grotesque half-faces hovering over me, random collections of features that changed and changed again.

Do you know where you are?

No—but at some point I began looking about for clues. Hospital, I said early on, but that wasn't good enough.

Gradually I came to understand that at the end of each night shift someone wrote the new day's date on a whiteboard at one side of the room along with the physician, RN and NA assigned that shift, so pretty soon (with no idea what *soon* in this circumstance might encompass) I had that much covered.

Progress.

Good boy.

They were *so* pleased.

Over time, too, I learned to fake recognition of staff members, and to look for the hospital's name, which I never could keep hold of in my mind, on nametags.

Yep, I know where I am all right.

And it's the 21st. (Though if they pushed for day of the week I foundered. That wasn't on the whiteboard.)

Seizures? I answered. Stroke?

Then the questions got harder. After which they said let's go for a walk why don't we, an absurd goal given my inability to turn unassisted in bed or move my legs, the physical therapist's verbal commands meeting with no greater success in converting directive to action than those coursing along my nervous system.

This page currently unavailable.

Please try again later.

Error.

But I needed ambulation to qualify for further rehab. So therapist Abraham sandbagged me into sitting position, hauled me to our feet and, with mine dragging and scraping at the floor, carried me the required half dozen steps, the unlikeliest dance partners ever.

We were on our fifth, maybe sixth provisional government by then. Some were ill-advised, rapidly-imploding coalitions, so . . . five, six, seven, who can be sure? This one had begun to look as though it might stick, like the stray cat that follows you home and, once fed, stays.

I learned that later, of course.

Three worlds, Abraham said, coexist. There was the old world of things as they are—of acceptance, of discipline, where we take what pleasure exists in what we have and expect no more. There was the new world, in which everything, country, selves, the world's very face, becomes endlessly reinvented, remade, refurbished. And now this third world struggling to be born, where old world and new will learn to live with one another.

Like Abraham and myself scuttling across the hospital's tiled floors.

I'm not supposed to be talking like this, Abraham said.

We were on a break, and he'd pushed me outside, to a patio bordered by scrubby bushes and smelling of rosemary, where with minimal help I'd successfully tottered from the wheel-chair and stumbled five terrifying steps to a bench. Applause would have been in order.

I asked if reinventing myself was not what I was doing.

More like rebuilding, he said. Refurbishing.

When I was a child, living in the first of our many homes, money was aflow, families and the neighborhood on their way up. If you tore a house down entire, you had to apply for new building permits. Leave one wall standing, it could pass as a re-model. So crews arrived in trucks and on foot to swarm over the site, piles of roofing, earth, brick and siding appeared, and with-in days, where the Jacobs or Shah house had been, there stood, in moonlight among hills of rubble, the ruins of a single wall.

Ready to get back to work? Abraham said. Patiently they await: Leg lifts, stationary cycling, weights, countless manifes-tations of pulleys and resistance. Row . . . Pull . . . Hold . . . Hold. Stepping over minefields of what look like tiny traffic cones. Balancing atop a footboard mounted on half a steel ball. Both of those last while clinging to walk bars and waiting for the state to wither away as Abraham said the old books predicted.

But five weeks further in, buckets of sweat lost to history, I've still not progressed past totter, trip and hope like hell I'll make it to the bench. A convocation gets called. The physician I've taken to thinking of as Doc Salvage is spokesperson. Here's the story, he begins. He smiles, then puts away the smile so it won't get in the way of what he has to say.

They fully appreciate the work I've done. My attitude. My doggedness. My determination. They know I've hung on like a snapping turtle and refused to let go. The consensus is that we (pronoun modulating now to first-person plural) have gone as far as might reasonably be expected. In short, I can stay as I was, with severely diminished capacities, or.

Or being that I undergo an experimental procedure.

They would reboot and reconnect synapses, restore neural pathways, rewire connections that had failed to regenerate autonomously. And while they were in there they'd go ahead and rearrange the furniture. Spruce things up here and there. New carpet, fresh paint.

You have the technology to do that? I asked.

We do.

And I'll be myself again, physically?

A better version. Though we understand (the smile is back) that sentimentally you may be attached to the present one.

And what of risks? Complications?

Oh, nothing terribly untoward. More or less the standard OR checklist: bleeds, infection, drug reactions. A long recovery.

You've all this certainty, with an experimental procedure?

Life itself is an experimental procedure. As you know.

And I've already had a long recovery.

Ah, that. Fundamentally you will have to start over, I'm afraid. Begin again.

And so I did in subsequent months as Doc Salvage and crew watched closely to assess development and as I pushed harder at my limits than I'd ever have thought possible. We were down in the swirly deep, in the sludge, as Abraham deemed. But within weeks the leg that before could scarcely clear the floor now could kick higher than my head, I could hop across the room, steady as a fence post, on a single foot, and fingers could pick bits of straw from off the table top. I could climb, crawl, swim, run, lift.

And wonder at what I'd been told, what I'd not.

You've taken note, Doc Salvage said six months later, how little resistance there is for you in physical activity.

Uncharacteristically, window shades were up behind him and light streamed in, so that he appeared to have a halo about his body, or to be going subtly out of focus.

All much as we anticipated, he said. But it is far from being the story's end.

He paused, letting the moment stretch. Something reflective passed outside, a car, a copter, a drone, tossing stabs of light against the rear wall.

Our bodies teem with censors built and inculcated into us, Doc Salvage continued, censors that create distraction, indecision, delay—drag, if you will. Morality. Cultural mores. Emotions. Most particularly the last. And we have learned how to bypass those. Eliminate the drag. We can peel away emotions, mute them, dial them down to the very threshold.

As, he said, we've done with you.

Which explained a lot of what had been going on in body and mind, things I'd been unable to put into words.

I now fit, they believed, a container they'd made for me.

But already, even then, I was spilling from it.

◁

They had given me something. They had taken something. On such barter is a society founded. How much control over our lives do we retain, how much cede to the state? What debts do we take on in exchange for the state's benefits? How does the state balance its responsibilities to the individual and to the collective? To what degree does it exist to serve, to what degree to oversee, its citizenry?

Theories grinding against one another in the dark.

The truth is this: Our enemies at the time were messing about with neurotoxins. It was those neurotoxins, not a CVA, not seizures as I'd been told, that came upon me in the burned-out fields of the far northwest. Those upon whose reach I was borne to the government hospital to awaken empty, blank, and helpless, isolate fragments of the world cascading around me.

The truth is this as well: I was changed. By the gas. By Doc's procedure. By the experience of reinhabiting my own body. And later, by my actions.

Only with time did I come to understand the scope and nature of the changes within. Doc was right that emotions no longer obscured my actions; about much else he was wrong.

A single image remains from before medics scooped me up. I am dragging myself across stubble. I can hear nothing, feel nothing. My legs refuse to function. And all I can see—this fills my vision—are my arms out before me. They stretch and stretch again. Each time I pull my body forward, they stretch more. My hand, my fingers, are yards away, meters, miles. And I do not advance.

But within a year of that meeting with Doc Salvage I was on the move. There was much, in this fledgling nation, to be done.

◿

The lamentations of old men forever fall deaf on youngster's ears, my uncle said. He knew that early.

Sometimes I imagine myself an old man tied by sheets into my chair in the day room of a care center speaking—even though there is no one listening, no one there to listen—about the things I did, things I refused to do, things I never quite recovered from doing.

At a table nearby, two men and a woman play cards, some game in which single cards get dealt back onto the table. In at least ten minutes no one's put down a card. It's the woman's turn. The men sit unmoving, hands before them, cards fanned. They could be mannikins propped there. On the screen across the day room a giant face says she loves us, in the same movie that plays at this time every Tuesday, but no one cares.

How does one assay right and wrong? With change crashing down all around us, do the words even have meaning?

Is everything finally relative?

What would you give, Sid Coleman used to sing, *in exchange for your soul?* An old, old song.

I know that the world of which I speak sitting here tied into my chair would be unrecognizable to the young. Unrecognizable to most anyone, really, should they chance to be around to hear. And as I speak, I watch cockroaches scuttling on the wall, lose my thoughts, begin to wonder about the cockroach's world. They've been around forever, never changed.

All this, of course, knowing that I will never be an old man.

4.

"This is your place?"

"Borrowed. Property is theft—right?"

Out on the farthest edge of the city. Forager territory. Dog-pack-and-worse territory. I looked about at the cot, racks of storage cells, plastic units stacked variously to form furniture of a sort. All of it graceless and functional, the sole concession to domestication being a plaque hung on a side wall and jiggered to look like an old-time sampler: *Always Drink Upstream of the Herd.*

"You can't be here often, or for extended periods. What happens when you're not?"

"I have guard rats." He began pulling cubes from one of the stacks. "Joking. About theft and property, too." He reconfigured the cubes as a chair, more or less. "Those who live out here and I have an understanding. Turns out we've much in common."

"Being?"

"That you deal with an unfree world by making yourself so free that your very existence is an act of rebellion. Camus, I think."

"Yet you run with the marshals of that world."

"Their screens, drones and watchers catch most of what happens on the surface of their world. But much goes on beneath, in ours."

"Giants of the deep?"

"Minnows and small fish. Thousands upon thousands of us. Where the true history resides."

Li pulled a link from his pocket, punched in.

"The villagers want to climb the hill and storm the castle, and there is no castle. The castle is all around us. What we have to do is learn to live in it."

As he spoke, perfectly relaxed, he was sweeping and scanning at impressive speed. "Ever come across a series of children's books, *Billy's Adventures*?"

I shook my head.

"I read them when I was five, six. The first one started off: 'Two years it was that I lived among the goats. Two years that I went about on all fours, ate whatever came before me.' Like most kid's books, as much as anything else they were put out there as socializers. Teach the boys and girls how to get along with others, shore up received wisdom, hip-hurrah things-as-they-are. But scratch the surface and what was underneath gave the lie to what was on top. The books weren't about joining the march, they were about staying apart while appearing to fit in. They were profoundly subversive."

Back when this area was a functioning part of the city, Li's squat had been a service facility, a utilities satellite maybe, a goods depot. Layers of steel shelving six- and eight-units deep sat against the rear wall. Stained and worn cement floors, splayed heads of ancient cables jutting from the wall. Steel everywhere, of a grade not seen for better than half a century, including the door that now rang open to admit an elderly man in clothing at once suggestive of tie-dye and camouflage. Balding, I saw as he slipped off his cloth cap.

"And so here you are back with us," the man said. Trace of a far-northern accent in his voice. "And not alone."

Li introduced us. "Thank you for minding the burrow, Daniel—as ever."

"Well then, we can't have just anyone moving in here, can we? We do have standards." Then to me: "Welcome to the junkyard."

Li had continued to monitor his link as we spoke. Now he beckoned me. The screen showed a street in the central city, masses of people moving along, dodges, feints, near-collisions.

"There," Li said. The cursor became an arrow, touched on one individual moving at a good clip close to storefronts and walls. "And there." Two larger figures, perhaps six meters back, matching speed with the first. "I'm piggybacked on security feeds. Seconds ago, sniffers at the corner dinged."

"Those two are armed."

We watched as the lone figure turned into a narrow side street or entryway. Both pursuers hesitated at the mouth, then stepped in, first one, then, on a six count, the other. People streamed by on the sidewalk. We waited. Moving at an easy pace, the single, smaller figure emerged. Patently she'd taken note where the cameras were and kept her face averted, but size and carriage were unmistakable.

Fran.

Molly.

"By now she's in the wind and the area's spilling over with police."

"And those hunting her will have new dogs in the area along with them," Li said. "Unless, of course, they're the same." He thumbed over to news feeds. No mention of the incident. Then to the city's official feeds, where delays from technical problems had been reported in the area and citizens were advised to consider alternate routes. "So many multiple realities," Li said. "Is it any wonder we're unable to see the world straight on?"

◢

Time passed, as it will, however hard one holds on.

Li told me about religious practices among the Melanese who during old wars and due to the island's tactical location, grew accustomed to airplanes arriving almost daily filled with goods, some of which got shared, much of which got cast off and reclaimed. For many years after, with that war over, the islanders carved long clearings like runways in the forest, built small fires along them to either side, constructed a wooden hut for a man to sit in with wooden disks on his ears as headphones and bamboo shoots jutting out like antennae. They waited for the airplanes to return with goods. Everything was in place. Everything was just as before. But no airplanes came.

It began to feel as though what we were doing in our approach to the whole Fran-Molly affair wasn't far removed.

Why would Fran signal for backup then fail to make contact, even to make herself visible? Leapfrog, maybe? Assuming we'd move in and her pursuers' focus would shift to us, leaving her free to . . . what?

Look again.

There had been urgency, power, in that attack. The air crackled with it. Fran knew where cameras were placed, carefully kept her face averted. From visual evidence her pursuers also knew, yet took little effort to skirt the cameras. (1) They were protected or (2) They didn't exist.

And just what did we hope to learn by endlessly reviewing the incident? "One works with what one has," Li said every time we thumbed up the file.

What we had was next to nothing.

And hellhounds on our trails. We could all but hear them snuffling around out there in the dark.

5.

Government after government fell, each trailing in its wake the exhausted spume of grand theories. Anomie had come piecemeal over so long a time that we were hard pressed to remember or imagine another way. Platitudes, slogans and homilies had supplanted thought. That, or unfocused, unbridled hatred.

Was the government at which we arrived a better one, or were we simply too exhausted to go on? The bigfish capitalism we fled and the overseer government we embraced had much the same disregard for bedrock democratic principles. But each individual was housed, educated to the extent he or she elected, provided sustenance and medical care, state-sponsored burial.

Border disputes, blockades, financial sloughs, outright attacks, the collapse of alliances. Those early years thrummed with dangers to which our nascent union, fussily jamming the day, often reacted with little regard for long-term consequence.

Ever on the go, the world's contours shifting and reshaping themselves even as I passed among them, I grew accustomed to media and official reports of a world far removed from that I witnessed. Which among these gaping disparities were sinister, which utilitarian? And just what was it I was doing out there? The people's work? The government's? That of a handful of wizards behind the curtain? One of Sid Coleman's songs comes to mind again, "Which Side Are You On," not all that much of a song really, but a damned good question. I wonder every day.

I was a good soldier, as soldiers go. One would expect years of such service to fix in place conventional, conservative beliefs. Instead, they honed within me an innate aversion to authority and to organizations in general. When I rummage in the attics of my mind, what I come up with is an immiscible regard for personal and civil liberty.

⊿

Claeton, pronounced Claytown by locals, mid-January and so cold that when your nose dripped, icicles formed. A thick white mist rose permanently from the ground. Bare trees loomed in the distance, looking as though someone had strung together a display of the hairless legs and knobby knees of old men. We inhabited a ghostly sea bottom.

Hansard and I were squirreled down in a scatter of boulders where a mountain range ran out into flatlands. There was one pass through the range and a patrol from Revisionist forces was on it. We were waiting for them.

Everyone knew the satellites were up there, circling tirelessly, bloated with information. And if satellites monitored even this afterbirth of a landscape, I told Hansard, they had to be watching us as well—not us here, us everywhere. Hansard shrugged and squeezed a nutrient pack to start it warming.

Drones might have dealt with the patrol, of course. Quickly. Efficiently. But drones hadn't the dramatic effect of a couple of warriors suddenly appearing at the mouth of the cave. Something in our blood and ancestral memory—others of our kind come for us.

Hansard finished drinking his nutrient, rolled the pack into a compact ball and stuffed it in a cargo pocket. The wind rose then, mist swirling like huge capes, cold biting into bones. Go codes buzzed in the bones behind our ears.

◁

We couldn't pronounce the name of the place but were told it translated as Daredevil or Devil-May-Care. Biting cold had turned stewpot hot, barren landscape to cramped and crowded city. The stench of used-up air was everywhere. You could smell bodies and what they left behind. Sweat mixed with fine grit, pollen and laden gases and never went away. It coated your body, a hard film, a second skin that cracked when you moved. Hansard, rumors said, had gone down up here near the Canadian border some weeks before.

That time, we almost failed to make it out, beating a retreat through disruptions turning ever more chaotic (dodging raindrops, an old Marxist might have said) hours before the region tore itself apart, this being what happens when a government eloquently tottering on two legs gets one of them kicked out from under.

◁

They came for us on the bullet train in Oregon. I turned from the window where sunlight shone blindingly on water, blinked, and there they were. Boots, jeans, Union jackets with the patches torn off. I've a brief memory of Tomas aloft, zigzagging towards the car's rear on the backs of the seats, right foot, left, starboard, port, before I turned to confront the others. All became in that instant clear and distinct. I could see the tiniest bunching of a muscle in the shoulder of one before that arm moved, see another's eyes tip to the left before head and body followed, sense the one about to bound directly toward me from all but imperceptible shifts in footing and posture.

I remember condensation on windows from the chill inside the car, the wide staring eyes of a child.

Afterwards, we liberated a pickup from a parking lot nearby and rode that pale horse into Keizer to be about our business.

⟁

Years after that day in Oregon, and as many after what I'm recounting here, Fran and I stand where Merritt Li died. In those years, wildness has reclaimed that edge of the city. Sunlight spins toward us off the lake to our left as though in wafer-thin sheets. Spanish moss beards the branches of water oaks populated by dove and by dun-colored pigeons that were once city birds. Fran touches another oak near us; scaly ridges of its bark break off in her hand.

We're the only ones, she says.

Who will remember, I say.

It's become rote now.

No memorials for such as Merritt Li.

Only memory.

For another who has been erased. Who has been gathered. And for a time before Fran speaks again, we are quiet. Our voices drift away into the call of birds, the sough of wind.

Our kind were redundant before and will be again.

As the successful revolutionary must always be, right?

Okay. She laughs. *They can be redundant too.*

A heron floats in over the trees and lands at water's edge. A heron! Who would have believed there were herons left? I see the same light in Fran's eyes as in mine. Still, after all that has happened in our lives, we have the capacity for surprise, for wonder.

6.

When I was eleven, a contrarian even then, I made a list of all the stuff I never wanted to see again on TV and in movies. Wrote it out on a sheet of ruled paper, signed and dated the document, and submitted it to my parents.

People jumping just ahead of flames as house, car, pier, ship or what-have-you explodes.

The disarming of bombs with everyone else sent away as our hero or heroine sweatily decides which wire to cut.

Police or soldiers putting down their guns in hostage situations.

Hostage situations.

The cop, finally pushed to his/her limit, tossing badge or detective's shield onto his/her CO's desk.

The cast, be they doctors, lawyers, or cops, all striding side by side, often in slow motion, along a corridor on their way to another fine yet difficult day as credits roll.

"I wanted to give back."

"This is your chance to do the right thing."

"You're not going to die on me!"

How with two minutes left in the show the bad guy tells us why he's done all he has, that it's all justified.

The original screed ran two pages. In following years, amendments—additions, truthfully—added another fourteen, growing ever more prolix until attentions strayed elsewhere. From time to time as I submitted new editions, I requested progress reports from my parents. Could he have been so innocent, that fledgling contrarian, as to believe some channel existed whereby they might actually deal with these issues? Was he attempting to bend the world to some latent image he had in mind? Just to shout out to the world: *I am here*? Whatever else it may have presaged, the project attests that at least, even then, I was paying attention.

By this time I'd got heavily into reading and may have had at the back of my mind, like that movement in the room's corner you can't locate when looking straight on, intimations of how powerfully words affect—how they give form to—the world about us.

I became aware that my greatest pleasure lay not in what was happening within the confines of the narrative but in its textures: the surround, the moods and rhythms, the shifting colors. And that it was auxiliary characters I found most interesting. A quiet rejection of celebrity, maybe—this sense that those spun out to screen's edge, the postmen, foils, second bananas, loyal companions and walk-ons, are the ones who matter? History with its drums and wagons and wars marches past, and we go on scrabbling to stay in place, huddled with our families and tribes, setting tables, trying to find enough to eat.

Sheer plod makes plow down sillion shine, Gerard Manley Hopkins wrote. Not that, when you come down to it, we do a hell of a lot of shining. At best we give off just enough light to hold away the dark for an hour or two. That's all the fire Prometheus had to give us.

∠

Light was failing, if never the fire, as Merritt Li and I made our way on glistening streets, cleaving insofar as we could to shadow and walls. Rain had begun hours earlier. Streetlights shimmered with halos, windows wore jackets of glaze—as would lens. That gave small comfort at the same time that the fact of fewer bodies abroad gave caution.

We weren't following leads so much as what someone once called wandering to find direction and someone else called searching for a black hat in a pitch-black room.

Rain made a rich stew of a hundred smells. Took away edges and corners and the hard surface of things. The city was feeling its way towards beauty.

There did seem to be a rudimentary pattern, the attacks moving outward from city's center, but patterns, what's there, what's not, can't be trusted. Apophenia. The perception of order in random data. See three dots on an otherwise blank page, right away you're trying to fit them together. Nonetheless, we were trolling in rude circles towards the outer banks, touching down at rail stations, pedestrian nodes, crossroads and terminals of every sort. That amounted to a lot of being out there in the open, exposed, and as chancy for Li as for me at this point, but (returning to a prior observation) what else did we have?

In such situations, while outwardly you're alert to every small shift or turn, changes in light, in movements around you, your own heartbeat or breathing, inwardly you're floating free, allowing your mind to do what it does best unpinned. Thoughts skitter, burn, and flare out, some shapeless, others barbed. As I scurried from sillion to sillion, bench to stairway to arcade, thoughts of childhood, books, folk songs, populism and political exhaustion accompanied me.

All I wanted was for my life, when you picked it up in your hands, to have some weight to it, Fran once told me. Rain coming down then outside our TBH as it was now on city streets, the two of us waiting for nightfall and go codes, foxhole reeking of processed food, stale air, unwashed bodies.

Within months of that, the GK virus had carved away fully a sixth of our population, especially among the elderly, infants and the chronically ill, all those with compromised immune systems, poor general health, low physical reserves.

Explanations for the virus? Natural selection at work in an overpopulated world, willful thinning of the herd by intellectual or financial elitists, Biblical cleansing, our own current government's research gone amiss, biologic agents introduced by any of a dozen or more current enemies.

Or that old friend happenstance.

Substantive as they were, Li's and my excursions had yielded little more than an anecdotal accounting of the city as it stood, along with instances of kindness, cruelty, anxiety and insouciance in fairly equal measure, in every conceivable shape or form.

Crews were busily tearing out the forest of digital billboards at city center, these having recently been judged (depending on the assessor) unaesthetic or ineffective.

The dry riverbed, cemented over years ago, was now being uncemented on its way to becoming a canal complete with boats and waterside city parks. Government-stamped posters with artists' renditions of the final result hung everywhere. Those of a cynical disposition well might wonder where funds for this massive project originated. More positive souls might choose not to take note of the disrepair in surrounding streets.

Repeatedly as we moved through the city we encountered flash-mob protests. Participants assembled without preamble at rail stations, on street corners, in the city's open spaces. Most protestors were young, some looked as though they'd awakened earlier in the day from Rip Van Winkle naps. They'd demonstrate, sometimes with silence and dialogue cards, other times with chants or improvised songs, and within minutes fade back into the crowd, before authorities showed up.

"We're chasing shadows at midnight," Merritt Li says one day.

And I hear Fran, another day, another time, saying "We're the shadow of shadows."

We'd come in country under cover of night, the two of us, and trekked on foot miles inland. The sky was starting to lighten and birds to sing when we reached the extraction point. Joon Kaas had not spoken a word the whole time, from the moment we breached his room. He had looked up and nodded, risen and gone ahead of us when signaled to do so. Now at the clearing he lowered his head, to pray I think, before meeting Fran's eyes (instinctively aware she was prime) and nodding again, whether in surrender or some fashion of absolution I can't say.

"He knew," she said after.

That we were coming. Of course he did. And how it had to end.

Later I would understand that for most of his countrymen, thousands of them cast onto the streets and huddled together in houses, the eternally poor and forgotten, those without influence who went on scratching out a bare subsistence as terrible engines fell to earth all around them, Joon Kaas was a savior. With his passing, much of what he had worked to put in place, his challenges to privilege and to authority, new laws and mandates, new protections, began one by one to disappear.

◁

Perhaps more than anything else, we've enslaved ourselves to the grand notion of progress. In our minds we've left behind yesterday's errors, last year's lack of knowledge and crude half measures. Now we're headed straight up the slope, getting better and better, getting it right. But really, we go on hauling along these sacks of goods we can't let go of, can't get rid of, tearing apart our world only to rebuild it to the old image.

In 1656 Spinoza was excommunicated from Amsterdam's Portuguese-Jewish congregation for inveighing against those who promoted ignorance and irrational beliefs in order to lead citizens to act against their own best interests, to embrace conformism and orthodoxy, to surrender freedom for security. This, even though Dutch society had long agreed upon liberty, individual rights and freedom of thought. Four hundred years down the road, not much has changed. Same hazard signs at the roadside. Same crooked roads.

◁

It was in the last months of the struggle, while I was over the border in Free Alaska commandeering armaments, that I first felt the gears slipping. Four degrees coldly Fahrenheit outside. With a wind that felt to be removing skin slice by micrometric slice. Fortunately I was inside, and alone, when it happened, having just entered a safe house there. I remembered walking in and stepping towards the bathroom. Now I was on the floor, with urine puddled about me. How long? Five, six minutes by my timer. Vision blurred—a consequence of the fall? Taste of metal, copper, in the back of my throat. And I couldn't move.

That was far too familiar, a replay of week after week in rehab, frantically sending messages to legs, arms and hands that refused to comply, Abraham urging me on.

I doubt the immobility lasted more than a minute, but hours of panic got packed into it. I began to remember other stutters and misfires, each gone unremarked at the time. Now they took on weight, bore down.

"What are you thinking?" Fran will ask not long after, on our visit to Merritt Li's final foothold.

"An old sea diver's creed," I tell her, unsure myself of the connection, thinking of the fighters we took down there, of Merritt Li going down, of my own fall and my jacked-up system, "the one thing a diver forgets at great peril: If it moves, it wants to kill you."

Then I tell her what happened at the safe house, what it means. Simple physics, really. Put more current in the wire, it burns out faster.

"When did you know?"

"From the first, at some level—wordlessly. One sleepless morning in Toledo I got up, tapped in, and pulled the records. I wasn't supposed to be able to do that. They had little idea what I could do."

I, the soft machinery that was me, was failing. Sparks failed to catch, messages misfired, data was corrupted.

I had, I supposed, a few months left.

7.

We never knew how Merritt Li came to be there.

His and my courses were set so as to bring the two of us together, close enough to rendezvous anyway, every three hours. When he didn't show at the old waterworks, I went looking. We both carried ancient low-frequency 'sponders we thought wouldn't be tapped. Guess we were wrong. They knew I was coming.

He had two of them back against a wall of stacked, partly crushed vehicles, tanklike cruisers from the last century. Two others, halfway across a bare dirt clearing hard as steel, had turned away to intercept me. Where numbers five and six came from I have no idea, they dropped out of nowhere like Dorothy.

A couple of them had weapons we'd never seen, the kind that, if you go looking, don't exist. Focused toxin's my guess. Or some fry-brain electronic equivalent. I saw nothing, no muzzle flash, no recoil, no exhaust, when one of those locked on Li lifted his handgun, but I saw the result. Li went down convulsing, limbs thrashing independently as though they belonged to different bodies.

Three of the four coming for me fell almost at the same time, one down, two down, three, without sound or obvious reason. Once I'd dealt with the fourth and looked again, the two by Li were on the ground and still. The whole sequence in just under sixteen seconds.

Movement atop a battered steel shed to the right took my attention, as it was meant to do.

Never show yourself against the sky.

Unless you're purposefully announcing yourself, of course.

She came down in three stages, over the side and catch with the left, swing to the right, drop and turn. Faultless as ever. No sign of what weapon she'd used. I recalled her late interest in antiquities, blowpipes and the like. One violinist wants shiny new and perfectly functional, another's always looking for old and funky, an instrument that makes you work to get the music out.

Her hair was cropped short and had tight curls of gray like steel filings in it. The row of geometrical earrings, circle, square, triangle, cross, was gone from the left ear. Otherwise not much had changed. Musculature stood out in the glisten of sweat on her skin. Yellow T-shirt, green pants.

"Interesting choice of clothing for someone doing her best to be invisible."

"Figured if it came to it and I stood dead still, they might take me for a vegetable."

Blood had pooled in Li's face, turning it purple, then burst in a scatter of darker splotches across it. Limbs were rigid. No respiration, no pulse. A pandemic of that: No pulse or respiration in the ones she'd put down either.

"Here we go leaving a mess behind us," I said.

"Ah, well."

"With a bigger mess waiting ahead."

"Ah, well again." She snatched the mystery weapons from those by Li. "We hit the floor with whoever shows up on our dance card." Then looked around. "No eyes out here. No trackers."

"Chosen for it. So they're not government."

"Who can say?" At the time we believed them to be a single team, didn't understand there were three factions at work, a tangle of forces.

Fran had dropped to a squat and was breaking down one of the weapons. "Indications are, they think of themselves as freedom fighters. Then again, who doesn't? Freedom from taxes, bureaucracy, using the wrong texts at school? Or maybe they just want to tear the house down. Maybe we should have asked them."

She stood and brought over the gutted weapon. "Ever seen a power source like that?" A bright blue marble with no apparent harness or connection, spinning gyroscopically in a chamber not much larger than itself. "Have to wonder what else they have."

"Six less footmen, for a start."

"There'll be backup. We should be missing."

"Missing, we're good at."

"Have been till now."

She retrieved the second weapon and we started away. Darkness had begun unfurling from the ground and the air smelled of rain. Insects called to one another from trees and high grass, invisibly.

"When I was a child," Fran said, "no more than four or five, there was a cricket that sang outside my window every night.

I'd go to bed, lie there in the dark and listen to it sing, night after night. Then one night it didn't. I knew it was dead, whatever dead was, and I cried."

Fran as a child, crying, I could scarcely picture. "Why were these six, and the others, on you?"

She pulled the power source from the first weapon, discarded its carcass. "They weren't."

She'd been working a private job much like that of mine back before the team in dark gray cars came for me, and stumbled onto something that wasn't right. She finished the job and took to side roads, kicking over traces till she realized that both job and not-rightness were come-ons. Hand-tied lures, she said, designed to bring her out. So out she came. They were stalking her. She was stalking them, coming in and out of sight. Getting a fix on them. Who they might be, how many.

"They were moving around in teams, randomly, and about where you'd expect, train stations, transfer points. They'd see me, hang back, never close. Which was how I knew it went deeper. So I stepped it up."

"And they stepped in."

"Maybe they got impatient. Maybe like me they decided to push to see what pushed back. And I sent a message up the line to you—which is what they anticipated."

By this time we were moving towards the central city but on back streets long forsaken, block after block of abandoned warehouses and storage facilities from a past in which people were driven to accumulate so much that it spilled over. We'd spotted a few stragglers of the kind that, once seen, quickly vanish. Tree dwellers brought to earth, I think of them, on the ground but never quite of this world.

8.

A razor-cold January morning. Snow falling past the windows—silently, but you can't help looking that way again and again, listening. How could something take over the world to such degree and make no sound? The room's warmth moved in slow tides toward the windows, tugging at our skin as it passed by. Even the machines were silent as I did my best to become one with them.

Abraham watched and paced me, speaking in low tones about Ethical Suicides back during our string of interim governments.

"Not much there when you go looking . . . Loosen up, I can see your shoulders knotting . . . Barely enough information to chew on . . . Breathe. Everything comes from the breathing . . . ."

I'd often wondered how a man with such leanings could possibly wind up working where he did. Were his intimations a furtive challenge, a testing?

"This is difficult for us to grasp, but you have to look back, to the sense of powerlessness that got tapped into. People were convinced that government, that the country itself, was broken and couldn't be repaired. They saw an endless cycle of paralysis and decay about which they could do nothing. ES's were not about themselves, they were about something much larger."

I stopped to catch breath and shake muscles loose. Took the water bottle from Abraham. Eager electrolytes swarmed within. "Absolute altruism? In addition to which, they acted knowing their actions would come to nothing?"

"That's how it looks to us. To them, who can say? Can we ever appraise the time in which we act?" Abraham stacked virtual weights on the upper-body pulleys, thought a moment and dialed it down a notch. "You're skeptical."

"Of more and more every day."

"With good reason." He reached for the water bottle at the very moment I held it out. *Another dead soldier* had become a joke between us.

Shortly thereafter, as had become our custom, sheathed in featherweight warmsuits, we were walking the grounds. Snow still fell, but lightly, haltingly. "When I first came, not so many years ago," Abraham said, "there were still dove in the trees, calling to one another. It was the loneliest sound I'd ever heard."

The rehab facility had originated at city's edge, adjacent to a cemetery with old religious and older racial divisions, then, as the city burgeoned, found itself ever closer to center. The cemetery was gone, doves too, but bordering stands of trees and dense growth remained.

Further in towards the heart of the complex sat the original building about which all else had accrued, three storeys of rust-colored brick facade and clear plastic windows that on late evenings caught up the sun's light to transform it into swirling, ungraspable, ghostlike figures. Other times, passing by, I'd look up to see those within, on the second floor, peering out, and feel a pull at something deep inside myself, an uneasiness for which I had neither word nor explanation.

It was Abraham who took me there late one night. *The colony*, as he put it, *is sleeping, Nessun dorma.* Entering, we passed up narrow stairs and along a corridor with indirect lighting set low in the walls, then to a single door among dozens. There was a scarred window in the door and in the window, still as a portrait in its frame, a face.

"This is Julie," Abraham said.

The woman's face turned slightly as though to locate the sound of his voice. Her eyes behind the glass were cloudy and unfocused. They didn't move, didn't see. After a moment she shuffled back away from the door, obviously in pain, perhaps remembering what had happened other times when voices came and the door opened.

"Surely you must have known," Abraham said. "You had to suspect."

That scientific advances do not happen without experimentation, and that experimentation walks hand in hand with failure?

So much gone deeply wrong with this woman, so many failures in the world that put her there.

9.

Most of the rest you know, or a version of it. You live in a world formed by the rest. You also believe you had some say in the making of that world, I suspect, and I suppose you did, but it was a small say, three or four words lost to a crowded page. There's a long line of wizards behind the curtain vying for their turn at the wheel. When Fran and I floated to the top one more time before sinking out of sight for good, whatever grand intentions might have been packed away in our luggage, truthfully, we were doing little more than the wizard's work. Can we ever appraise the time in which we act? Probably not. How do we decide? With a wary smile and fingers crossed.

It was Abraham who called out to me, and to others like me with whom he had worked over the years. Abraham, who once carried me across the room as though I could walk, to qualify me for rehab. Abraham who never hesitates to remind us that we stagger from place to place, day to day, beneath the moral weight of acts we didn't commit but for which we are responsible. That in allowing ourselves collectively to think certain thoughts we risk damaging, even destroying, the lives of millions, yet surely, if any of this means anything at all, we must be free to think those thoughts, to think *all* thoughts.

Never forget it's because of such men as Abraham and Merritt Li that you have the life you do, with its fundamental rights and fail-safes.

Try always to remember the responsibility that comes with those freedoms.

The easy part of government? Ideals. Rational benevolence.

The hardest? Avoiding the terrible gravity of bureaucracy, the pull away from service towards self-survival.

Max Weber had it right over a century ago.

Not much time left for me now. What came to the fore in that Alaska safe house has run its course. I can feel systems shutting down one by one, like lights going off sequentially from room to room, hallway to hallway. The overloaded wire burning down. I'm intrigued by how familiar it feels, how welcome, a visit from an old friend.

Fran is here waiting with me.

Opposite my bed there's a window that for a long while I took to be a link screen as in it I watched people come and go, out in the world, I thought. Couples strolling, crowds flowing off platforms and onto trains, scenes of towns like Claeton, like those in Oregon. Children playing. But that couldn't be right, could it?

I am eight. I have no idea as yet how much heartache is in the world, how much pain, how it goes on building, day by day. I have a new toy, a two-tier garage made of tin, with ramps and tiny pumps and service pits, and I'm running my truck from one to another, making engine sounds, brake sounds, happy driver sounds. On a TV against the wall at room's end, videos of war machines flanked by infantry unspool as a government official inset upper left reads from a prompter saying that high-level talks are underway and that we expect—

And that can't be right either. I'm imagining this, surely, not the garage, the garage was real, but the crash of that newscast into my reverie . . . Am I dreaming? It's harder and harder to tell memory from dream, imaginings from hallucination. Harder and harder, too, to summon much concern which is which, to believe it matters.

All in a moment I am that child with his garage, I am pulling myself along with impossible arms after the toxins take over, I am struggling to stand and stay upright in rehab once brought home from the battlefield and yet again after the surgery, I am driving deserted highways at 10:36 on Union Day.

Fran leans close, her hand on mine. I see but cannot feel it. As she will not hear the last thing I tell her. That we go on and on and, all the time, terrible engines whirl and crash about us, in the great empty spaces that surround our lives.

Acknowledgments

How the Damned Live On first appeared in *Asimov's Science Fiction Magazine*.

Miss Cruz first appeared in *The Magazine of Fantasy & Science Fiction*.

Ferryman first appeared in *Borderland Noir*, ed. Craig Mcdonald.

Freezer Burn first appeared in the anthology *CrimeFest 2018 (UK)* ed. Adrian Muller.

Bright Sarasota Where the Circus Lies Dying first appeared in *Welcome to Dystopia*, ed. Gordon Van Gelder and John Oakes.

The Beauty of Sunsets first appeared in *Alfred Hitchcock's Mystery Magazine*.

What You Were Fighting For first appeared in *The Highway Kind*, ed. Patrick Millikin.

Dispositions first appeared in *Ellery Queen's Mystery Magazine*.

Billy Deliver's Next Twelve Novels first appeared in *Xavier Review*.

Figs first appeared in Ellery Queen's Mystery Magazine.

Sunday Drive first appeared in *Bound by Mystery*, ed. Diane DiBiase.

The World Is the Case first appeared in *Louis Vuitton: Fashion*

& Travel.

Zombie Cars first appeared in *Grey*.

Net Loss first appeared in *Analog*.

Season Premiere first appeared in *Dark Delicacies II*, ed. Del Howison and Jeff Gelb.

As Yet Untitled first appeared in *Asimov's*.

Comeback appears here for the first time.

Beautiful Quiet of the Roaring Freeway first appeared in *Interzone*.

New Teeth first appeared in *Analog*.

Scientific Methods first appeared in *North Dakota Quarterly*.

Annandale first appeared (under the title Bedtime Story) in *The Magazine of Fantasy & Science Fiction*.

Dayenu first appeared in *Lady Churchill's Rosebud Wristlet*.

About the Author

Jim's previous books include eighteen novels, multiple essay and story collections, a biography of Chester Himes, a translation of Raymond Queneau's novel *Saint Glinglin*, and five collections of poetry including *Black Night's Gonna Catch Me Here* from New Rivers Press. He's received a lifetime achievement award from Bouchercon, the Hammett Award for literary excellence in crime writing, the Deutsche Krimipress, the Brigada 21, the UK's H.R.F. Keating Award for criticism, and the Grand Prix de Littérature policière.

About New Rivers Press

New Rivers Press emerged from a drafty Massachusetts barn in winter 1968. Intent on publishing work by new and emerging poets, founder C.W. "Bill" Truesdale labored for weeks over an old Chandler & Price letterpress to publish three hundred fifty copies of Margaret Randall's collection *So Many Rooms Has a House but One Roof.* About four hundred titles later, New Rivers is now a nonprofit learning press, based since 2001 at Minnesota State University Moorhead. Charles Baxter, one of the first authors with New Rivers, calls the press "the hidden backbone of the American literary tradition."

As a learning press, New Rivers guides students through the various processes involved in selecting, editing, designing, publishing, and distributing literary books. In working, learning, and interning with New Rivers Press, students gain integral real-world knowledge that they bring with them into the publishing workforce at positions with publishers across the country, or to begin their own small presses and literary magazines.

Please visit newriverspress.com for more information.